June 2019

To Carmen & Carmen!

Hold Every Moment Sacred

Love,

[signature]

By Cathy Chavez

ISBN: 978-0-578-49522-4

First Edition: April 2019

For information contact:
Cathy Chavez
cthychv@aol.com

Book and cover design by:
Mary Wright
Quills, Nibs, and Keyboards Editing and Design Service
http://www.qnkediting.com

CONTENTS

Dedicated in loving memory to

Brandon, Candace, Cariana, Lee, Liana,
Mark, Patrick, Priscilla, and Susan

Introduction

My left hand felt her strong heartbeat through the thick layers of her soft flannel pajamas. It gave us a connection that would last forever. I believe everyone, including my husband and some of my brothers and sisters, in the room that night could actually hear her heart beating. At the same time that her powerful heartbeat gave us hope, we all knew it was her way of saying goodbye.

My mother's heart stopped beating at 4:30 on the morning of December 11th, 2009. That date will always have an attached meaning that I cannot forget. Whenever I see the date, it triggers a connection to her. Sometimes it's the expiration on a milk carton or a yogurt label.

I used to save them, but due to space issues, I had to stop. I smile now when I see it, even though it was the worst day of my life. Many people tell me that I was lucky to have her die in my arms. I didn't feel lucky. I found myself remembering all of the things I would say to the parents of my patients who had died, and I felt very foolish. There was nothing anyone could say to make them feel better, and now I realized that first hand. I wanted the world to be quiet, to shut down, as I had. To just *stop!* But as the song says, *"The world didn't stop for my broken heart."* I felt incredibly weak and helpless.

Facing that day was impossible. I tried to go to sleep at my daughter's house, but all I did was toss and turn as I forced myself to face my life without parents. My father had died in the very same bedroom almost twenty years before that day. Despite the fact that I was surrounded by my family, it was a very lonely morning preparing to head home. I remember hesitating at the door when I realized I would never enter her house again and find her there. I felt that my soul needed some grounding before I could go on living. In my mind, I thought that perhaps if I went home with my husband and prepared a meal in my own kitchen, I would feel strong and solid again.

My sister, who hadn't been to my house in over ten years, decided to go home with us. It was a good thing because my plan to ground myself failed miserably. As I was rolling tortillas, the tears started to fall. They wouldn't stop. I found myself on the kitchen floor sobbing and sobbing, in a place anyone who has lost someone dear to them is all too familiar with. My husband helped me to the couch, and my sister finished the so-called "grounding meal." She had to finish making tortillas for us and rolled them out very thick. My husband later made me laugh for the first time that day when he referred to her tortillas as "fatties." I have always been fond of his keen sense of humor.

That day certainly set the tone for my new life and encompassed the deepest loss that my heart had ever felt. I suppose I had come to understand what loss was. At the same time, I would begin to understand what it would take to survive the loss. The two things that continue to help me move forward in a positive way are that I am not alone, and I can laugh again.

The story you are about to experience is an attempt to describe grief and loss through the lives of different women. It is also going to illustrate what they found to be helpful in their survival. This is a story about small acts of kindness and true patience. The healing that takes place for these women starts off as magical and grows through a lifetime.

Part 1

San Francisco

Early Twentieth Century

Chapter 1

Inocencio Sanchez was San Francisco's 20th mayor. He came from a large family of dedicated farmers and owned thousands of acreages in San Francisco including 1,000 acres of land directly facing the Pacific Ocean. The views from this area were and still are breathtaking. Despite his great love for farming, Inocencio had other passions that he somehow found time for. He loved to read and collect books and could never go anywhere without a book in hand. Many times, he would leave the books where he had been working. It was rumored that every year at harvest time, the family would find upwards of 100 of Inocencio's books in the fields. For some miraculous reason, the books were always found in perfect condition despite their exposure to the elements. Inocencio's close and devoted friend, Joaquin, always took it upon himself to collect the books in a wheelbarrow and return them to the barn that substituted for a library at the time. Joaquin had built shelves in the barn on every wall to house Ino's books.

Inocencio's wife, Theresa, who referred to him as "Ino," never bothered him about his obsession with books. One day when they were first married, she had learned by accident why he felt such a connection to his books. It was during one of the pre-harvest days when she asked Joaquin to bring that day's collection of books to her kitchen. She glanced through several of them and discovered that most had page numbers written at the top of the last page. She then turned to the corresponding pages, where she discovered the cause of Ino's attachment to his books. It brought tears to her eyes.

Ino's mother, Francine, had died of tuberculosis in the house in which they now lived. Theresa had always encouraged Ino to spend time with his mother while she was still alive, as she was old and a bit frail. Francine was also quite fond of books. When her eyes failed to allow her to read, Inocencio would read to her. It became a common sight to see the two of them sitting outside on her porch as Inocencio read to her.

After his mother died, the first book Ino attempted to read brought him a gift he would never forget; a small miracle that he believed to be from Heaven. It was there, in writing, on page 191 of a mystery book. Francine! His mother's name in print! It brought tears to his eyes, but at the same time, an amazing peace took up residence in his heart. Her name was the name of a character in that book, but it also appeared in other books. Sometimes it was the name of a hospital, a ship, or a hurricane. Once it was even the name of a large tent in a store! Every time he saw her name in a book, Ino believed that his mother was sending him a sign from Heaven that she was okay. He would always go to the back of the book and write the page number where her name appeared for future reference. It was just another chance to see his mother's name in writing. Somehow that gave him the courage he needed to move forward in life. He would never forget her name. His books were precious to him. Later in life, he came to refer to them as his friends.

That day when Theresa discovered the connection between her husband and his books, she quietly accepted his obsession of searching for one more sign that his mother would never leave him. Although they never spoke of the "book miracle," Theresa now realized that Ino wanted other people to experience their own miracles through books. He was always looking for ways to bring peace to people living with the pain of grief. His chosen way of sharing books with everyone was to build a public library. He dreamed of it existing in the middle of North Beach in San Francisco. He wanted it to contain old and rare books of all types and subjects, and for everyone to have access to them.

Inocencio died one year prior to his dream of opening the public library. His family saw to it that on December 11th, 1923, The People's Library opened its doors. It still stands in the center of North Beach. There have been many accounts of sightings of Inocencio in the library. The locals tell stories of experiencing visits and even talking with a very soft-spoken man who directs them to read books that have opened their hearts to peace. It is not unusual for the bereaved to visit the library in hopes of a healing. The healings are described as "visits" from loved ones who have died, and present themselves in the form of their names or of special dates found in the books. Of course, the library is always well stocked with tissues, as tears are such an important part of healing. It is believed that unshed tears often occlude grief and can work against it.

Chapter 2

San Francisco 1902

Books weren't the only method of healing that Inocencio is remembered for. On April 2nd, 1902, the Sanchez Bath House was opened to the public. It was located on land that Ino owned, facing the Pacific Ocean. His dream was to make the bathhouse available to all people. Enclosed in a magnificent building were the world's largest heated sea water pools. The pools were surrounded by bleachers that could hold nearly 5,500 spectators. There were dressing rooms to provide swimmers privacy. Swimmers could enter the water by swinging in on huge ropes or even slide in on one of 15 slides. The second floor had many small coffee shops and restaurants for the public.

On opening day, the weather was very stormy. Clouds appeared off and on, and the threat of rain remained throughout the day. Inocencio was still putting final touches on the short distance railway he had to build to make it possible for people to reach the bathhouses. The entire city of San Francisco was excited about this day, except for Ino's wife. Theresa claimed that she was worried about Ino's health. Inocencio had been diagnosed with diabetes several years earlier and was notorious for cheating on his doctor-recommended diet. His favorite snack was doughnuts, and he had already consumed three that morning. Theresa was furious. She loved her husband dearly and only wanted the best for him. But her two daughters knew her well enough to have recognized that something else was responsible for her troubled mood this morning. When Inocencio had first discussed his bathhouse dream to Theresa years prior, she had immediately dismissed the idea that this dream would ever transpire. Why would anyone find joy in swimming? What a ridiculous idea, Ino! She refused to be a part of this dream of his. Throughout the years it took to build the Sanchez Bath House, Theresa remained in a state of denial, refusing to even discuss the subject with Ino. She kept herself busy and distracted in the beautiful flower garden that she had created on their property.

One afternoon, Ino stopped for coffee at his mother-in-law Margarita's house and brought up his current bathhouse project. That morning he learned something about Theresa's family that he had never known, despite their years of marriage. Margarita shared with him that Theresa had an older brother named Rudy who had died of a drowning accident when he was ten years old. Theresa was four years old at the time, and it had happened in the ocean near Point Lobos. It became more and more apparent to Ino that his mother-in-law felt responsible for her son's death. Her grief as she described it to him was inconsolable because she was riddled with guilt. She cried as she said over and over again that if she had not allowed her son to go swimming that day, he would still be here.

Later that day when Ino told Theresa what he had learned, she opened up to him about her brother's death. Her loss, as she described it, was more about losing her mother. She could recall her mother sobbing uncontrollably as she would walk on the beach near the ocean. Margarita rarely smiled after the death of her son, and she refused to have her picture taken. She cared for Theresa in a responsible, protective way, but always seemed distant. For Theresa, her mother died that day right alongside her brother. Theresa remembered feeling as though she attended two funerals on the day they buried Rudy; one for her brother and one for her mother. Her mother would never be the same, as she had attached herself to a new companion in her life called guilt, which would keep her forever sad and distant to all who loved her.

As life would have it, Inocencio forged on with his dream. Something seemed to drive him even harder now that he had learned of Theresa's family's loss. It became a passion of his to find a remedy to this impossible pain that existed within Theresa and her mother. He desperately wanted

Theresa to see her mother smile again and for Margarita to let go of that controlling companion called guilt. Ino believed that a healing had to occur to rid Theresa's mother of that guilt. Perhaps somehow the seawater pools could help. Theresa only pushed her silent sorrow deeper into her broken heart. She came to support her husband with his bathhouse dream, but at the same time wanted no part of it. After all, it was water that had caused her brother's death and her mother's guilt.

Chapter 3

Spring 1902

"Don't forget to bring extra clothes and our matching parasols, Vivien!" Candace shouted.

The Sanchez girls were seven years apart in age but were simply inseparable. They grew up knowing that they were a part of every important event that took place in their parents' lives. The opening of the Sanchez Bath House was one of the most outstanding events of the spring of 1902, and the Sanchez home was simply lit up with energy and excitement. It would take at least two hours to travel by train from downtown San Francisco to the Sanchez Bath House. The opening ceremony was to take place at noon. Inocencio had planned to meet the girls and Theresa at the train station. The Sanchez family would then travel together from the train station to the bathhouse.

Despite the conflict that Theresa felt in her heart, she knew how important this was to her husband. It felt impossible to her that any healing that could take place in the water. Her brother's drowning had taken place over twenty years ago, but in her heart, it felt like yesterday. She tried desperately to erase the memories of her mother's sorrowful crying, but was unsuccessful. The only way she was to survive this day was to stay incredibly distracted. It was not uncommon for Theresa to create distractions in her life in order to erase grief. This particular distraction was perfect. She had easily talked Inocencio into allowing her to set up a fresh flower shop on the promenade level of the building. It would be alongside of the coffee and gift shops that were located there. The shop would require many hours of dedication and the work put her in a state of constant exhaustion. What a great way to avoid grief! Theresa was no stranger to planning what she needed to survive in life. She had purposefully chosen a location for the flower shop that faced the opposite view of the swimming pools, yet still allowed her to view the ocean and its incredible calming beauty. Flowers brought smiles to just about everyone. What a wonderful gift Theresa was about to experience. Perhaps she planned to receive all of the forgotten smiles that her mother had found it impossible to give to her. She couldn't wait to open up the flower shop at the Sanchez Bath House.

Meanwhile, Candace and Vivien, or Vivi, as they called her, had decided to model the matching swimsuits they had bought for opening day. The blue and white striped suits were typical of swimsuits for 1902 and were exactly the same as the ones belonging to at least half of the other girls at the pool. Nobody minded because it was a great way to confuse parents as to their girls' whereabouts.

Concerts were arranged with free admission for all on opening day. The feeling in the huge bathhouse was that of open happiness and freedom. The glass-enclosed pavilion allowed natural light from outdoors into the area.

Months of planning had gone into the design of the pools. Seawater from the ocean waves went into a catch basin to filter out sand and seaweed. The clarified seawater was then pumped into an adjacent powerhouse. The powerhouse warmed the water to a comfortable temperature for the swimmers. At the pedestrian entrance, there was a huge grand staircase which descended from the promenade level to the swimming pools. Theresa's Flower Shop was conveniently located on the promenade. The humidity in the air helped her flowers stay fresh and healthy.

Inocencio and Theresa barely caught site of each other for moments at a time on opening day, but they both knew that something special was about to transpire. They knew that their love for each other and their families could only grow as a result of this endeavor. They knew that everyone experiences loss in life and wanted healing for all. There were no cures for a broken heart, but something magical would soon make its way into the Sanchez Bath House.

Part 2

Twenty Years Later

1922

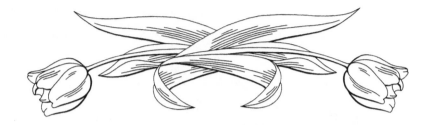

Chapter 4

Theresa was frightened when the bells at St. Peter and St. Paul's church began to toll. They seemed louder than usual at Inocencio's funeral service that Saturday morning in the Autumn of 1922. Perhaps it was simply that she was in a state of desolation over what was happening so quickly in her life. Inocencio had died a week ago, and Theresa could not ground herself to this new life without her precious partner. It wasn't the responsibilities that he had always taken care of, or even the financial burdens that they had shared that scared her. It was not having him there to talk to in the morning over coffee. That time had been so special to both of them, as it had given them both the strength they needed to face

17

the day. Theresa's mother had died eight years prior, and the pain was just beginning to lighten in her heart. *How many times can one heart break?* she asked herself.

The flower shop at the Sanchez Bath House had been closed for two weeks. Theresa's older daughter, Candace, reminded her that people were counting on buying flowers as gifts and she really needed to open up the shop.

"Maybe next week," Theresa said. "I'm just not ready," she whispered to herself.

It seemed as if everyone else knew what was good for her, but she certainly didn't feel it! There were moments when she thought her heart might stop beating, but it didn't. Life, in that rude way, just kept going on. The flower shop would definitely distract Theresa from her broken heart, but she didn't want to be distracted. She didn't want anything to get in the way of her great sadness over losing Inocencio. It was hard enough to accept the fact that all references to Ino were now in the past tense. As each day passed, time also created more distance to memories of him. That state of desolation that she had felt was disappearing and reality was here to stay. How was she going to go on living without Inocencio?

Meanwhile, between her two daughters, their husbands, and Theresa's four grandchildren, someone would visit her daily and keep her occupied. Steven, who was Vivi's husband, had taken over the day-to-day business at the bathhouse while Inocencio was still alive, so he knew firsthand what Ino's dreams for it were, especially as pertained to decisions that had to be made about its future. He was an engineer by trade, so he was perfect for the job. Theresa appreciated his serious manner and careful way of making decisions. Vivi and Steven's sons, Patrick and Daniel, were following in Steven's footsteps and often accompanied him to work.

Candace's husband, David, managed the railway spur. He had been involved in the project from the very beginning and Ino had taught him everything he knew about the short railway that connected San Francisco to the Sanchez Bath House. The upkeep of the railway and the bathhouse was expensive, and they always seemed to be in arrears financially. Inocencio's family was determined not to close the Sanchez Bath House. Both of Ino's sons-in-law had promised him that they would do everything possible to keep them open to the public. One compromise they had made was that they would be closed on Mondays and Tuesdays. This helped a little and actually worked out well for everyone.

The family all worked there in one capacity or another and saw each other quite often. Through the years, they had got to know the bathhouse regulars and treated everyone with respect. The public appreciated that personal touch and encouraged others to visit.

Candace, Theresa and Inocencio's oldest daughter, taught swimming lessons in one of the hidden and quieter pools on Wednesday mornings. For some reason, no one had signed up for the next session that was scheduled to start in the Fall. Candace decided to advertise the slot as an All-Women's Swim Group from 9:00-12:00 just to see what would happen.

Still, she wondered. *Will anyone show up? Will I find myself, two weeks from now, all alone, listening to the echoing water in the pool?* She couldn't imagine what would happen in this unpredictable time in her life. She missed her father every minute of the day but was afraid to even mention that in front of her family. It was Inocencio's spirit that gave her courage, and she was holding on to it for dear life.

Sanchez Bath House
All Women's Swim Group
Wednesdays 9:00a.m.-12:00
Inquire within

Chapter 5

Rose

Rose had been waiting over thirty minutes outside the flower shop, hoping it would open soon. She desperately wanted some perfect, red, June roses for Jacob's grave, and she knew that the best June roses were always sold at the flower shop at the Sanchez Bath House. The mere thought that he was all alone at the cemetery caused a pain so deep in her heart it almost knocked her down. The only thought that she could keep in her mind today was the idea of replacing her middle son's wilted flowers with fresh red roses. It may have sounded strange to some people, but for Rose the plan in itself would temporarily ease her pain and had given her a reason for getting out of bed that day. The flower shop was still closed! Her only hope for surviving that day was beginning to fade when all of a sudden two gorgeous women came rushing up the stairs in front of where Rose was standing. They were carrying so many flowers, it appeared that the flowers were floating towards her on their own! The sight of that made her laugh out loud, something she hadn't done in months. It was as though her prayers had been answered and the flowers were literally flying to her! The shop would open up soon. For almost thirty seconds, Rose felt what it was like to be happy and smile again, an impossible feeling these days.

Candace immediately began to explain why they were late.

"I am so sorry we are just getting here! I feel terrible about this!" she said in her most apologetic voice. She wouldn't normally share personal information with customers, but this woman, for some reason, seemed to be very understanding. Maybe it was the sincere manner in which she listened.

"I'm Candace, and this is my sister, Vivien, and our mother usually runs the flower shop. Our dear father passed away and, well, our mother just can't get going. That horrible saying people keep repeating that 'life goes on...' is starting to become a reality for us. We decided to open up the shop for her today," Candace said, her voice quivering.

"Can I get you a cup of tea? We have some delicious Chamomile Lavender that we just got!" Vivien chipped in as she sensed her sister's weak spirit.

"Sure, that sounds great, thank you. I'm Rose, by the way."

Once they had explained to her the reason the shop had been closed lately, Rose understood immediately and offered her condolences. She wouldn't say, 'sorry for your loss.' Instead, she gave them each a gentle hug and whispered a prayer for them. She had become an expert in what not to say when trying to comfort someone who had suffered a loss. After her nineteen-year-old son Jacob had died, so many people had said such

24

ridiculous things to Rose that she no longer reacted to the comments. She simply ignored them. Deep inside, she knew that people meant well and couldn't really hurt her any more than she was already hurting. It did, however, create a distance between her and most of the world. They didn't understand how she was feeling. One person had actually said, "Don't worry Rose, you still have two other sons." That was something she would never repeat to anyone.

****

The only other people who knew exactly how she felt were Leroy, Joseph, and James, Jacob's father and two brothers. They had all been close by when Jacob took his last breath that dismal fall. He had been confined to his bed for the last six months, and had actually felt like he was a part of his bed for the last three. He had died due to severe damage that a rare cancerous tumor had done to his spine. That morning, September 4th, Leroy had begun the heartbreaking yet satisfying ritual of shaving Jacob for the last time. Leroy sensed that Jacob was fading into a distant place that he could no longer be a part of. He loved his son and would have done anything to trade places with him. He gave him a perfect shave in the most loving way he knew how. This gave him a special memory that both broke his heart and revived it every time he recalled that morning. That time belonged to him and Jacob and was something no one else had.

****

The red roses Candace chose for the bouquet that morning at the flower shop were perfect. Some of the buds hadn't opened yet, but looked very promising for the next week or so.

"I can't thank you enough for putting together such a lovely bouquet, Candace!" Rose knew that her trip to the shop had not been a waste of time. She told Candace that she wanted to order the same arrangement for the next week. Candace, of course, agreed, and invited Rose to the all-women's swim group that was to start the next Wednesday. Rose immediately hesitated, as she had never been much of a swimmer despite the fact that they had a pool at their house in the Mission District. The boys had spent countless hours swimming in the pool when they were growing up and many times had forced Rose into the pool. All three of her sons were notorious for throwing people into the pool.

"Maybe I'll come. Well, I don't know. But for sure I will come for the flowers next week." Rose hadn't felt this much energy in months. She felt so excited as she walked with pride carrying Jacob's red June roses. *I suppose he would want me to swim here next week but I really can't plan that far ahead in this strange new life,* she thought to herself.

Meanwhile, Candace's eyes had filled with tears as she thought about where the bouquet that she had prepared was going. It only reinforced the thought that her mother needed to keep the shop open and running. She had decided that she would not mention this morning's encounter with Rose to her mother, as she was afraid of saying anything that might make her cry. Candace feared Theresa's tears. She had no idea that there really wasn't anything that could upset Theresa more than what she was already feeling from losing Inocencio. The story might have even made her mother feel comforted by the love Rose had for her son. But that was the story of Theresa's life now. Everything said to her by others was filtered and predictable. People were constantly trying to shield her from sadness. She longed for honesty, but it felt like everyone was so busy "protecting" her that she was all alone.

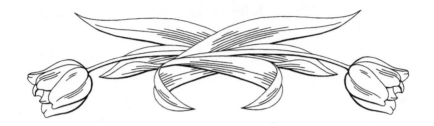

Chapter 6

Early in Inocencio and Theresa's marriage, they had decided to give both of their daughters land near where they lived in San Francisco. This would make it possible for them to build their own homes with their own privacy, yet still have them close by. Neither of them could fathom the idea that their daughters might move far away, so, just as planned, once they were married, both Candace and Vivien built homes close by on the land that their parents had given them. Fortunately, their husbands, Steven and David, had agreed to live close by. There were so many benefits in that arrangement. For example, mealtime was often shared amongst all of them. They referred to them as 'community' meals. Sharing food meant sharing love, Theresa believed. She remembered that Candace and Vivien had always been all about sharing.

There were times when the girls were little that had seemed ridiculous. For example, Candace had always despised egg yolks. She was forever leaving them behind on her plate, on her desk, or even on the couch! This had made Theresa furious!

"Candace! Is this another egg yolk of yours? Why do you continue to leave them all over the house?" Theresa would scream.

"Oh mom, please. It's just a little yellow ball. What's the big deal?" asked Candace.

Vivien, the family peace-maker, who loved eating but hated shouting, decided that she would follow Candace around the house whenever she ate eggs and retrieve the egg yolks. Vivi thought they tasted very good and decided that she would simply pick up after Candace and eat her abandoned egg yolks. What a simple solution to the problem, she thought in her precious three-year-old mind.

Candace always taught Vivien new things about life. This included reading. Of course, Ino supported this and would bring children's books home all the time and the girls were always excited to read them.

****

Presently, in the 1920's, the Sanchez girls were all grown up and had families of their own. It was very reassuring to know that the support they gave each other and to Theresa was mutual. Help was always right around the corner if anyone needed it.

Chapter 7

Lily

Lily had decided months ago that when her parents came to her graduate school graduation in San Francisco they would celebrate by going to her favorite Mexican food restaurant in the Mission District. She even knew what dress she would wear for that day. It was a soft peach color with gold buttons that created a beautiful contrast with her shoulder length dark brown hair. Her mother had made it for her. They were the same size, so it had been easy for her mother to make her clothes even though she lived far away. She also knew Lily's favorite colors.

Lily's husband, Edmund, wanted to plan a party for her, but neither of them were sure if her Mom would even be able to travel after her recent brain surgery. Her diagnoses with a serious brain tumor had changed all the plans that Lily's family had made. Both Lily and Edmund had decided that a graduation party was out of the question. Things were changing fast, and that frightened Lily. She had just found out that she was pregnant and wasn't feeling well. One minute she was on top of the world, knowing in her heart that despite her previous miscarriage, this pregnancy was going to give her and Edmund a beautiful baby at last. The next minute, she felt scared out of her mind that her mother would not survive the brain tumor that lately seemed to be taking over their lives. Lily and her father talked constantly over the phone. Sometimes there were things that happened that Lily's father didn't even mention to her because there were more important and serious developments in her mother, Susan's, condition.

Being across the country from each other made things hard on everyone. Wisconsin had never seemed so far away. It broke Lily's heart not to be back home. She and Edmund hadn't even told her parents that Lily was pregnant. She was in a state of double prelude, one to happiness and one to grief. Her emotions were changing constantly. Lily thought that once they told her mother that their baby was due in December, it would lift up her spirits and maybe, just maybe, give her the hope and strength to survive.

The trip from Wisconsin went surprisingly well for Lily's parents. Everyone had agreed that a lunch at Lily's favorite restaurant was the best way to celebrate her graduation. While they were celebrating, Lily surprised her parents and told them that she was pregnant, and that they would soon be grandparents. Tears filled everyone's eyes, especially Susan's, Lily's mother. Once they returned to Wisconsin, Lily's father constantly reminded her mother that she needed to be strong enough to be around until December so she could meet her new grandchild. This seemed possible some of the time, but a tiny whisper in the back of Lily's mind was telling her that her dear mother would not make it to December.

No one in Lily's family had any idea how to handle this nightmare of a brain tumor that was dictating all of their lives. It seemed that almost on a daily basis someone said something outrageously insensitive and feelings were hurt deeply. There was one member of the family who had definitely won the prize for saying something stupid. It had been on one of Lily's trips to Wisconsin. Her mother had undergone surgery and Lily had traveled to be there afterwards. She had been studying at her desk while the rest of the family was in the main room of her parents' home. Cornelia, Lily's sister-in-law, entered the room uninvited and started a conversation.

"You know, Lily, if you continue to stress about your mother's diagnosis, you'll hurt your baby! You need to knock it off and take control of yourself!" she said, in her bossy and annoying voice. Lily simply ignored her, but deep inside she felt very hurt by that comment. She rolled her eyes, straightened her glasses, and continued to study.

Meanwhile, Lily's mom continued to decline and died courageously in September, three months before Lily was due to give birth to her baby girl. Once again, Lily was forced to live in a world of confusing and conflicting emotions. The only consolation was that she was not alone, and Edmund proved to be an amazing, supportive partner. He allowed her to grieve in her own way over the tragic death of her mother, Susan. Edmund also seemed to instinctively understand the loss of their daughter's grandmother, a hurt that is difficult to comprehend. Their baby girl hadn't even been born, yet had already lost her grandmother.

The loss of Lily's mother deprived her of the most trustworthy resource she had in her life. Mothers know everything about giving birth. Especially her's, because she had been a midwife. Lily longed to

31

ask her mother questions. She only felt doubt when she questioned her MD about things in her pregnancy. She tried hard to imagine what her mother would say, but only felt a deep silence in response.

Chapter 8

Theresa couldn't even imagine moving Inocencio's personal belongings, much less giving them away. She had refused to even wash the clothes that he had worn before he died because then they might lose his smell forever. She found herself caressing those clothes sometimes just to remember him. Never had she imagined how difficult it would be to go on living without him. It was definitely the hardest thing this life had asked of her. She didn't want this life anymore! It was too hard! Then her precious grandchildren would show up and make her smile again; a miracle in itself. Without even trying, the four of them always managed to show up at the right times.

"Grandma, we bought you some mangos!" said Vivien's son, Daniel. They were his favorite fruit and he was very anxious for her to help him cut one up.

"I never was very good at this Daniel, but I will give it my best because I know you are dying to eat it," Theresa said while putting Ino's favorite shirt back in her top drawer. She always had time for her grandchildren and would never ignore their needs and wants. Candace's twins, Silas and Sophie, would be following Daniel shortly and would ask her for another favor.

"Grandma Theresa, can we go for a walk? Mom said you would want that. Is it ok? Please, please, please?" said Silas.

"Please, please, please?" echoed Sophie. Soon there was so much commotion in the Sanchez home that the feelings of depression moved out of the way to make room for smiles and happiness.

Candace and Vivien soon walked into the house, only to add to the noise that was keeping Theresa's attention.

"Hi, Mom! How was your day today?" Candace said as she gently hugged her mother.

"Oh, it was good. I'm fine," Theresa whispered almost to herself. Candace and Vivi both knew the signs of recent tears on Theresa's face. Her eyes would get very red and she avoided eye contact. They both understood and were learning how not to ask why she had been crying.

"Mom, do you still know how to play the castanets?" asked Vivi with the intention of brightening up her mood.

"Why, yes, of course I do Vivi. Why do you ask?" said Theresa in a curious voice.

"We found a box with several pairs of them in the basement yesterday when we were looking for some of our old books. I want to give the books to the kids, so they can read them."

"Oh, I would love to see the castanets!" Theresa felt a sudden flood of memories of days when she would sit in the kitchen and watch her mother play the castanets. The sound of hard wood clicking came back to her immediately. And, of course, it was a time when her mother would smile as she wore her apron and danced around the kitchen, raising up her hands and clicking the castanets loudly. Theresa also recalled her mother's uncanny ability to snap her fingers very loudly! These were memories of happy times in Theresa's past. Both Candace and Vivien knew that Theresa's mood would transform once she began talking and remembering her mother. Hearing Theresa talk about her own mother was actually healing for the girls.

"What is a casta... casta-uhm...? What are you talking about, Grandma?" asked Sophie in her sweet, soft voice.

"It's called a castanet, Sophie, and my mother used to play them. They are like shells that are held together on the top with elastic, and you slip them on your fingers and click them together. I will show you and the others how to play them. We can have a castanet party!" Creating new memories with her mother's Spanish percussion instruments sounded wonderful to Theresa.

Staying busy with her daughters and grandchildren gave Theresa purpose in life. Nothing could take away her pain over losing Inocencio, but he wasn't the only person she had. She was not alone, that was for sure.

Chapter 9

Sunny

Life in the large house in the Bay Area couldn't get better for the Anderson family. Danny's new job with the Bureau of Investigation meant that his wife, Sunny, could quit her job as a real estate agent and spend more time with their first grandson. Their son, Brandon's girlfriend had given birth to baby Luke three years prior. He looked a lot like his father, the only difference being his beautiful blue eyes that charmed everyone who saw him. Not that Brandon didn't also charm everyone he met!

Danny would never forget the day Brandon was born. It was like falling in love again, only this time with his son. He was so thrilled that he actually hired a limousine to drive his beautiful blonde-haired wife, Sunny, and their new baby boy home from St. Amelia's Hospital that week. It was impossible to believe that now Brandon was a daddy, too! He was so proud of his precious baby. Luke adored his young father. Brandon brought many huge smiles to his little boy's face whenever he was around.

Now that he had a son to raise, Brandon felt the pressure to develop his profession. He had taken a job as a chef on a ship that made regular trips to Europe. That meant he would sometimes be gone for months at a time. This was very hard, but Brandon knew that he needed to support his son and provide for him in the best way he knew how. Hardly a day went by that Sunny didn't see her grandson. She was experiencing a new love for baby Luke that would soon be a source of survival for her.

Sunny and Danny both came from large families. They had four boys, including a set of twins who were the oldest. Then there was Brandon and the youngest was Martin. They spent holidays together despite the fact that the family had grown so large it was not easy to fit everyone in her house at the same time. Sometimes the teenagers would simply hang out in the backyard.

It was Christmas Eve,1921, and life couldn't have been happier. Danny was on an important case and couldn't be home that night but would be home in time for Christmas Day. Sunny had made him promise that he would come home the minute he was able. Brandon's ship was due to return in February, right after his birthday, so he would not be home for Christmas Eve either. This made Sunny sad, but she had hopes and kept distracted with baking hundreds of biscochitos. These were everyone's favorite cookies at Christmas time and took lots of effort to make just right.

It was 10:00 pm and the family had just finished exchanging gifts. Surprisingly, Danny arrived early and Sunny was relieved when she spotted him from across the crowded room. She had been cooking and baking all day and was very tired. One of their twin sons, Eric, motioned for both of them to meet him outside on the side of the house.

Once they were outside, away from the crowd of relatives, Sunny could see in Eric's eyes that something was very wrong.

"What is it? What's wrong?" she said desperately. Eric couldn't speak. It was as though he was crippled. His girlfriend, Hannah, finally blurted out the words that would stun both Sunny and Danny for years.

"Brandon is dead. He committed suicide on his journey home" said Hannah.

"No, no, that's not true. No. You have to be mistaken!" Sunny screamed. Danny immediately went into crisis mode and began calling his Bureau contacts to get to the bottom of this horrible rumor. So as not to frighten the children, the five of them quickly gathered their other three sons and exited the home where they had just finished celebrating the very last Christmas when they had been happy and normal. Their lives would now be divided into two periods: before and after Brandon's death.

Back home, the phone calls began. The news traveled quickly and before long Sunny and Danny's home was filled with more family. Everyone had a million questions floating in their minds, but no one had the courage to ask. Danny was only able to obtain the simple, hard facts, and those were that Brandon had been found dead in his loft on the ship and that it was likely a suicide. There was nothing gentle or understandable about that news. There wasn't even a note left behind to explain what had happened.

From that day forward, Sunny would always feel a disconnect to the rest of the world. It was especially difficult because outside their lives, everyone was celebrating Christmas with music and food and gifts. The Andersons wanted nothing to do with celebrating. They felt as though they were not a part of this world anymore because the pain in their souls was all they could feel. Time had cruelly stopped for them. It would be years before they ever felt like moving forward in life and Christmas had a new meaning for them.

When Sunny was able to sleep for a few hours, she would only wake up feeling like there had been a mistake. Maybe it was someone else, not their son. *No, not Brandon! No! No! No!*

Brandon's older brother simply fell to the floor and sobbed uncontrollably when he learned what had happened. Danny pushed forward and decided that the family would go together to Seattle where the ship had docked and bring their son home. He made that decision without realizing that this trip would bring the family together in a very loving way. A way that made them the Andersons. They were all hurting inside, yet able to still care for each other.

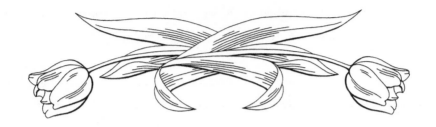

Chapter 10

"*I think mom is doing okay,* Candace, but I honestly can't handle it when I see her cry," said Vivien. "I feel so overwhelmed because I miss Dad too, and I feel like I can't tell her that."

"Well, Vivi, you know how Mom is. She knows everything, so you can't really hide your feelings from her. She knows we all miss him."

"Yes, you're right. Maybe we should talk about him more. I mean we're all thinking about him anyway," said Vivien.

"I think about him every day. In fact, just this morning I was remembering the time he decided to make breakfast for us. Do you remember that?" She laughed as she said this. Both of them immediately recalled one of their favorite memories of Inocencio.

It was 1910 and Inocencio and Theresa were on cloud nine, happily raising their two daughters, Candace and Vivien. Theresa had an old injury from an accident she was in as a child. She had been riding a horse that seemed to go crazy whenever anyone whistled. One of the neighborhood boys was trying to get her attention and had whistled loudly. Off Theresa flew, and landed on her hip. She had to be hospitalized for two weeks and was then on bed rest for another month.

Every so often as an adult, this injury haunted her in the form of a deep pain in her hip. It would actually knock her from her feet. Each time it acted up, she would have to rest for two or three days. This, of course, drove her crazy, as Theresa was used to taking care of all of the household duties, especially the cooking. It was a Saturday morning and Inocencio was up early, having his morning coffee earlier than usual because he wanted to surprise the family by making breakfast. This was something he had never done before.

The kitchen was "Theresa's department," he used to say. He was in a hurry because he didn't want his surprise to be spoiled. He grabbed a pan with a lid that he had spotted on the floor in the pantry where Theresa kept the potatoes. He carefully peeled the potatoes, washed them, and cut them into tiny pieces. He liked the potatoes cut very small, but Theresa liked them big. This was his chance to make them the way he liked them without hurting her feelings. As he stood at the stove, he felt very proud of the meal that he was making on his own. Sleepy-eyed Candace wandered into the kitchen and was soon followed by Vivien. The two of them eyed each other and began to giggle uncontrollably. After a minute, they were rolling on the floor laughing out loud. Soon they could hear Theresa calling out from the bedroom, asking what on earth was going on in the kitchen.

"Everything is under control, Theresa! I'm making a delicious breakfast for all of you," said Ino proudly. He was even wearing one of Theresa's famous aprons.

"Dad, Dad, Dad!" screamed Candace.

"What's wrong mija?" answered Ino in a very annoyed tone.

Vivien pointed to the pan he was cooking the potatoes in. Candace also pointed and said, "That's not a pan for cooking, Dad."

"Well, what kind of pan is it then?"

"It's Grandma Lujan's old basin!" shouted the girls in unison. "It's a toilet! Ha ha ha! You're cooking potatoes in a toilet!"

"Ay Dios Mio! Are you serious? I'm making the potatoes in a basin?"

Theresa finally wandered in and spotted the basin immediately. "Inocencio Sanchez, what are you doing?" Her eyes almost popped out of her head. "Oh, my goodness, this is a disaster! I feel fine! Please leave the cooking to me!"

Meanwhile, Candace and Vivien laughed until they cried. It became one of their funniest and favorite memories of growing up at home.

After recalling this memory, both Candace and Vivien decided that they should never stop telling "Dad stories" and that they should talk about their father in front of their mother from now on. Even if it brought tears to her eyes, it was important to keep him alive through their memories of him.

Chapter 11

Iris

Iris and Herman quietly carried boxes out of their home in Pacific Heights, San Francisco. This would be the last load of Herman's personal possessions and they would soon say goodbye to each other for the last time. They both wore dark sunglasses that day. It was better not to see each other's tears. There were no hateful words or spiteful wishes, they just would not, and could not, continue their marriage to each other any longer.

Four years prior, to that day their precious two-and-a-half-year-old daughter, Cora, had taken her last breath as Iris held her gently in her loving arms. Cora had spent most of her last months in Iris's arms. Iris found it very difficult to allow other people, including Herman, to hold Cora, as she knew her precious child would die soon.

Now the only thing she cradled in her arms was her grief. You never get good at saying goodbye, and Iris felt as though a pattern was forming in her life. She knew all too well what it would be like to face the mornings without Herman. Yes, her other two children would be a grateful distraction, but they could never take away the pain of loss.

Cora had been born with Down syndrome, but this never prevented Iris and Herman from having high expectations of their daughter. They were equal to the expectations that they had of Erin and Vanessa. When she was born, Dr. Winter told Iris and Herman that they would all outlive Cora, as the usual life expectancy of a child with Down syndrome in 1918 was only nine years. Iris immediately put that fact out of her mind and moved forward with a belief that Cora would outlive her. Unfortunately, the diagnosis of leukemia in Cora two years later proved them all wrong. This felt like more than just bad luck to them. This was beginning to feel like a punishment without a cause.

Iris and her family maintained hope for a miracle, but that soon faded when the doctors told them to expect Cora to die before summer.

"I have no doubt that this will be Cora's last spring," Dr. Winter had said as he quickly exited her hospital room. Her frail body matched the prediction. Iris found it impossible to comprehend how something like this could happen to Cora. She had been the happiest baby in the world. Fascinated with her many toys, and even learning to read. How could her life be ending? Silently Iris vowed to herself that she would make an effort to treasure every day with Erin and Vanessa. She had been true to her vow, as the kids were the center of her life.

Iris and Herman had both been aspiring journalists at the Chicago Times ten years ago. They had no intentions of having children, but then they suddenly had three! Back then, they couldn't have imagined moving across the country.

The *San Francisco Chronicle* needed a writer with an academic background and the sort of compassion and insight that came naturally to Iris. She had just been awarded a very prestigious award for the story she had done on Willem Einthoven, the Dutch Doctor who had invented the first electrocardiogram. He had received the Nobel Prize for it, and she had written an outstanding article describing exactly how it worked. Iris had always been fascinated with the heart and how it managed to beat so perfectly in the body. She also had a fascination with how a heart could stop beating.

****

They never admitted it, but perhaps the touch of competition with each other in their professions could have been part of the reason for their split. With her amazing skills, gorgeous auburn hair, and tall stature, Iris continued her work as a journalist. Herman, on the other hand, decided to leave journalism and go to Medical School to become an ER doctor. Fast forward ten years and they would both be lost in a world of similar, but separate pain. Their individual approaches to grounding themselves to life were unsuccessful. It was equally frightening for both of them to find a life outside of their marriage, but they knew that they could no longer hold on to their disconnected relationship.

Iris watched Herman drive away and somehow found herself sobbing in the bedroom that Cora was supposed to grow up in and redesign for herself as a teenager. Instead, the echoing room would remain suspended in time with her favorite toys, her forest green top, and her crib. Iris felt that suspension in time every day of her life.

Do people really move on, or is that a way of ignoring the bomb that just went off inside? she wondered. Moving forward sounded almost disrespectful to her daughter. What was she going to do with all of Cora's clothes? It had been four years since she had died, and Iris had gotten the impression from her family that no one would want the clothes of a child who had died of leukemia. Perhaps they feared their children would contract it if they wore her clothes. It was a painful thought that she would actually have to give her precious daughter's clothes to Goodwill. Iris had always been someone who helped those less fortunate, but she had a fear that she would lose connections to Cora with each of her donations. She didn't feel the same way about Herman's possessions, although he was pretty thorough in removing most of them.

Her job at the *San Francisco Chronicle* had required her to review miscellaneous articles on current events around town when she wasn't working on a story. That was just as well, because she still had absolutely no energy to be creative. She glanced quickly at the tiny article advertising an All-Women's Swim Group at the Sanchez Bath House.

Hmm, that sounds inviting in a strange and curious way. She circled the add and thought to herself. *Maybe I can go next week when the kids are with Herman.*

Chapter 12

Candace had no idea why Wednesday was her favorite day of the week. Everyone else seemed to dislike Wednesdays, but she very often woke up in the best of moods in the middle of the week. Her seven-year-old twins, Silas and Sophie often helped out at Theresa's Flower Shop. Silas' job was to make sure all of the buckets of flowers had plenty of water. It was common to find him taking long whiffs of the wonderful smells in the shop. Unusual for a child his age. The flowers were like friends to Silas. He would become very sad and even cry when he noticed flowers wilting. He knew that they would soon lose their strength and die just like his Grandpa Ino had. He would argue with his Grandma when she chose to throw out any old, wilted flowers.

"Grandma, these flowers are still alive! Look at them. See, there is still color in them and they are soft..." Silas would plead.

"And they are soft..." chimed in Sophie.

Theresa would find little piles of wilted flowers gathered carefully and placed in old vases on the east side of the shop. Inocencio had built Theresa shelves on that side for her to keep supplies such as extra vases and boxes. Silas was very comfortable wandering around that part of the shop.

Sophie, on the other hand, was more interested in managing the cash register. How she longed to be able to reach the huge counter where the cash register lived. That sharp clicking sound of it was magical to her. Both of the twins simply loved the time they spent at the flower shop.

Candace had planned that the first All-Women's Swim Group would start next week, however, despite the fact that she had strategically placed flyers everywhere in San Francisco, not one woman had signed up or even inquired about the group. Candace decided that she would still plan on opening the doors to the small pool, which was located near the back entrance to the bathhouse near the flower shop. Vivien promised her sister that she would stop by and encouraged Candace to proceed with her plans. "They will come. Don't worry," she said.

Hmm, Candace wondered. *Well, if nobody shows up at least I'll have time for a tranquil soak in the pool.*

Chapter 13

Lily: Recent Graduate

The silence of Liana's birth was deafening to everyone in the room that morning. Edmund was simply paralyzed. In the weeks before that morning, Lily was just beginning to feel the total absence of her mother since her death in September. And now, Baby Liana was gone. It seemed as though the people she loved the most in her life were disappearing way too fast.

On December 21st, Lily felt something changing. She was due to give birth soon, but her baby's little kicks seemed weaker, or perhaps less often; it was hard to tell at this stage of her pregnancy. The kicks against her tummy seemed almost ghostly. This was all new to Lily and she was losing her confidence by the minute. She found herself questioning everything going on in her body and didn't have her mom there anymore to ask her if this was normal or not. She couldn't determine the difference between her baby's real kicks inside her tummy or her own imagination. If only my Mom was here was a thought constantly arising in Lily's mind. Sadly, a deadly brain tumor had taken her mother to her final rest. Then on December 22nd – a day that will be forever etched in hers and Edmunds minds – it was confirmed by a doctor that their baby's tiny heart had stopped beating. The kicks that Lily thought she had felt were just fragments of a declining hope. Liana had died before she was born. How was that possible?

How could this happen? No! screamed the voice in Lily's mind. It was not until the next day that Lily actually delivered their baby girl, whom they lovingly named Liana. Despite knowing that Liana's heart had stopped beating the day before, Lily still held on to just a sliver of hope that they would hear her baby girl cry after she delivered her. The room was silent.

****

Lily and Edmund's hearts both went numb simultaneously. They now shared a nightmare of stillness that bonded them together forever in addition to their deep love for each other. They both found it hard to understand how something so horrible could hold them together, but in a strange way, it did. They each knew exactly how the other felt. Their loss was equal.

When it came time to plan Liana's funeral, three dates stood out. December 22nd, when Liana had died, December 23rd, when she had been delivered, and December 24th, when she had been due to be born. The last date always presented itself with hope, something that made Lily smile inside her quiet self. Even though they did not settle on a tombstone, Lily thought that perhaps all three dates would be on it. Once again, how does your precious baby die before she was born?

Chapter 14

Sunny

The weeks started to fly by, and soon it would be Brandon's birthday. Sunny and Danny had no idea how they would survive that day without him. What do you do when it's your son's birthday and he's not here to celebrate? It's still his birthday, right? But what do you do? Celebrate without him? Cry? Pretend it's just another day? Or do you tell people what day it is? Their world was so confusing now. Life had not prepared them for this constant mix of emotions. February 2nd was Brandon's birthday, but it felt as if he was disappearing from their worlds, even on his birthday.

For that matter, every holiday had the potential of turning into a disaster. Valentine's Day, Easter, Mother's Day, their own birthdays! Life presented constant reminders that Brandon was gone. Sunny felt that unless she planned some sort of event, she would never survive the day. She decided to plan a small gathering at a nearby park to acknowledge Brandon's birthday. Sunny had always been good at organizing events and delegating duties.

Now that she was a grieving parent, it felt strange not to have the same energy that always seemed to keep her going before Brandon had died. She did, however, have her two sister-in-laws, Lizzie and Janine. They lived in the same neighborhood and were like two crutches for her. One on each side! They held her up every day, and that was good. She needed the support that could only come from family.

"We can help put together a birthday celebration for Brandon," Lizzie said.

"We know that he will be here in spirit!" added Janine. That afternoon, Sunny felt relieved that she now had a plan for February 2nd and would surely survive with the help of family members who also missed Brandon and his sweet smile and contagious laughter.

It was a clear day and the birthday celebration was taking shape in the Anderson's backyard. Yes, there were tears, but there were also hugs and smiles to balance the sorrow. The family had written loving messages to Brandon on little pieces of paper and placed them in white balloons that were later filled with helium. The sendoff was beautiful.

"Danny, can I tell you what message I wrote to Brandon?" Sunny asked her husband that evening in their room after everyone left.

"Sure, I would love to hear it," responded Danny.

"Your story will never end..." whispered Sunny as they embraced each other.

****

56

The weeks turned into months, but even though time was racing by, the love and support from Lizzie and Janine did not disappear. It only became stronger.

Thanksgiving was just around the corner and once again Sunny felt scared and unable to cope. What would she do to survive the upcoming holidays? Little details about them became huge in Sunny's mind and nobody understood except for Danny! For example, who was going to give thanks at the Thanksgiving dinner? That was Brandon's job! He always gave thanks at meals in the form of a beautiful, thoughtful prayer. He always began with his shy smile and pronounced the words perfectly.

"Bless us, oh Lord, and these thy gifts which we are about to receive..."

Sunny could hear his voice as she remembered those words. There wasn't anything or anyone who could replace Brandon.

****

Lizzie was an avid swimmer and spent lots of time at the Sanchez Bath House. She had noticed the cute little sign advertising the All-Women's Swim Group that was to start up on Wednesday. That sounds like something Sunny may like, she thought to herself. Later that evening, she phoned her to tell her about the group.

"Hello Sunny? This is Lizzie. Do you have a minute?"

"Yes, of course, I always have time. Too much sometimes." She said in a sad voice.

"Well, last summer I participated in a co-ed swim class at the Sanchez Bath House and I really enjoyed it. I noticed a sign that is advertising an All-Woman's Swim Group starting up soon on Wednesdays. If you want, I would be willing to pick you up and drop you off on my way to the First Cake Bakery on Geary Street. I'm starting a baking class there next week."

The silence on the telephone made Lizzie wonder if she had made a mistake.

Sunny gazed at the photo of Brandon on her desk and then gently spoke. "Lizzie, how about if I think about that and then get back to you tonight?"

"I'll be here Sunny. I'll be here."

Click.

In that calm place inside her being, Sunny knew that Brandon would be there next Wednesday, in spirit.

She trusted Lizzie and decided after her suggestion that she might go to the swim group. She was certainly going to consider it. Anything to avoid worrying about surviving the upcoming holidays.

Chapter 15

Iris & Mark

On July 17th, 1921, the Sanchez family had made the decision to hire a very special young man to run the People's Library. Things were going well at the small library, but something was missing. It lacked the personal touch that Theresa remembered Inocencio talking about when he would dream out loud with her over morning coffee many years before. Theresa's two sons-in-laws were busy with the bathhouse and the small railway and simply didn't have the time to work at the library.

"I want everyone to feel at home in the library, Theresa... relaxed and comfortable. I don't want anyone to feel as though they need to rush off and read somewhere else," dreamed Inocencio aloud. This memory was powerful inside of her despite the fact that it was from twenty years ago.

The special young man that the Sanchez family decided to hire that July was Mark Fite Jr. He was short and thin and had a look on his face that made you wonder what he was up to. His gentle manner and sweet smile made him a perfect person for the job. Mark was proudly named after his father, who had been a General in World War One. He adored his father and had loved making him smile when he was a little boy by wearing his various uniform caps and shoes around the house. Mark learned how to salute at the very young age of three and had always been an eager reader. In high school, he took a job at Mission Lights Bookstore and had continued working there until recently, when his father was diagnosed with cancer.

It shattered his heart to learn of his father's diagnosis.

"Mom, there has to be a mistake! How can dad be sick? He is the strongest man I know. Strong people don't get cancer!"

"I know, Mark, but the doctors are quite sure. I'm going to need for you to help me care for your father," said his mother as she hid her tears. "Do you think you will be able to move back into our home?"

"I'll do anything for him, Mom, and you know that."

Slowly and carefully, he picked himself up and gathered all the strength he had within and bravely faced his life, ready and willing to care for the man he loved the most in his life. Financially, he needed a better job, so the opening of the People's Library was ideal. The hours were flexible, and he could still be close to books, which were his source of strength.

****

Iris often spent countless hours in the People's Library, doing research for the articles she would work on for the San Francisco Chronicle. Her job required utmost accuracy and she was a stickler about those things. Mark and Iris became great friends the minute they met. They seemed to be able to even finish each other's sentences when conversing. It wasn't uncommon for Vanessa and Erin, Iris' children, to meet her at the library after school, as it was right around the corner. Iris was comfortable talking to Mark and had shared with him that her youngest daughter Cora had died of leukemia several years earlier. The fact that Mark knew Iris had lost a daughter linked him to her past and he treated that with great respect. It gave him an understanding of the 'cloudy-like' melancholy that she possessed at times.

Chapter 16

Rose

Putting on rouge, black eye liner, and red lipstick in the mornings seemed to take longer and longer as the years went by after Jacob's death. Rose was a very attractive woman with long dark hair who always paid attention to details when it came to her looks. Somehow everything in Rose's life seemed to be measured by the day her son had died. Everything had a connection to that enormous loss.

Seven years had gone by, and time in Rose's life was different now. She no longer rushed around. If it wasn't for her career as a performer, she would probably never even leave the house. Life certainly took on a different pace for her. Fortunately, Rose had always loved to sing and was great at it. It came naturally to her. She worked at a small club in the Fillmore District that welcomed female Jazz vocalists. 'La Rosita', her stage name, found that even though it sounds impossible, she could cry and sing at the same time and nobody noticed. The dark setting in Jazz at JuJu's helped because it hid her flushed face and many tears. Rose had always preferred dark settings, and her powerful voice allowed her to scream out her sorrow over losing Jacob and entertain people at the same time. The grieving singer often wondered if anyone in the audience even had a clue about her deep sorrow.

****

It wasn't long after Jacob died that Rose and her husband grew apart and made the decision to divorce. They felt it was the best decision for everyone, so Rose and her two sons left the Mission District and moved to a small apartment near North Beach. The losses that happened in her life seemed to just exchange one pain for another in her heart. Which one will it be today she would often ask herself.

Singing the blues and Latino ballads took energy and strength, two things that Rose felt the most deficient in. Time had a way of dragging her along and forcing her to continue developing her beautiful talent. Band members would come and go, and Rose would find herself thinking about the fact that so much time had gone by that some newer band members never even knew that she had lost a son. They had never known Jacob.

"*Hola*, Rosita! How are you doing today?" Luis innocently asked Rose before band rehearsal.

"Oh, I'm okay. Just kind of tired... as usual," replied Rose.

"Oh, I see. I thought maybe somebody died, you look so sad." Little did Luis know that there was a somebody and his name had been Jacob. It had been seven years, long before Luis had joined their band. Rose felt like she just didn't have the words or the energy to explain her sorrowful look. She couldn't risk that other people might say something to give her the impression that they really were not interested in Jacob's death. That unbearable sadness taking up residence in her heart seemed about to explode into a million pieces. The only shred of hope for her survival that day was the fact that tomorrow was Wednesday, October 21st, and she would pick up another bouquet of June roses for Jacob's grave. Hmm, she thought to herself. Since I'm going to be there anyway, maybe I should just plan on staying for the All-Women's Swim Group that Candace would be teaching.

Chapter 17

Lily

Edmund had spent the weekend surfing at Point Lobos beach. Surfing was a way he had learned to make the pain go away temporarily. A powerful distraction. He had tried to convince Lily to join him, but she refused. She did, however, decide to meet him at the Seal Rock Inn restaurant for breakfast. They served her favorite pastries there, almond croissants. Trying out a different route to the restaurant would take her past the back entrance of the Sanchez Bath House. Wearing a large coat and a baseball cap kept Lily from being recognized by anyone that morning. She had lost so much weight after Liana's death that she had simply lost interest in her clothes. She wasn't in the mood to talk to anyone. She was certainly not in the mood for anyone to ask her about her baby and then have them cry or stare at her in that pitiful way that people did while they pretended to understand when she told them what had happened.

Lily had belonged to a bridge club that met every other Tuesday to play cards. Catching the trolley car and riding to the Presidio to meet several other women always gave her time to relax.

It just so happened that three of the other women had been pregnant at the same time Lily had been. All four of them would meet and discuss their plans for their children. They dreamed anxiously of a time when they could all meet at Crissy Field instead of playing bridge and show off their babies.

For Lily, that dream ended abruptly when Liana died. It was impossible for her to return to the bridge club. She wanted nothing to do with any of her friends, who were now busy spending time holding their precious babies. *How dare they want to talk to me?* she often thought to herself. *Don't they know I'm dying of pain from losing my precious Liana?* There was a time when she actually felt ashamed that she was had not been able to keep Liana alive. She understood that it was out of her control, but the guilt still haunted her.

****

Lily found it extremely painful to see even a stranger with a baby. Never even having the chance to hear Liana cry was a drowning sorrow that she couldn't get over. Her strong feelings even limited the books she was able read. If the story had a baby in it, she would toss the book into the fireplace. Edmund had attempted to retrieve several books from the fireplace. The look on Lily's face when she saw him try to do this once changed his mind in a second! He then tossed the painful reminders back into the fire. It just wasn't fair that the rest of the world had infants to care for and love and hers was gone. Simply gone without any memories other than the hopes and dreams that she had while she was pregnant. Those thoughts were also tainted by the impending death of her mother, which had occurred at the same time.

How could she lose so much in her life in such a short time? Her life had changed so drastically in the past year that she hardly recognized herself in the mirror. What happened to the attractive woman who fit perfectly into fancy suits and beautiful wool sweaters? Not anymore. *Who am I?* she often asked herself. *I feel like I am disappearing.* She felt lost most days and in a fog that never burned away by noon like the famous San Francisco mist outside.

As she was passing the back entrance to the Sanchez Bath House near the beach, she noticed a small sign:

All-Women's Swim Group
Wednesdays at 9:00 a.m.
Inquire within

She hesitated and then looked at her watch to check the time. The watch had been a gift from her mom. Lily believed that her mother gave the watch to her so that time connected them in some strange sort of way. She was an hour early and had plenty of time to explore. Exercise was important these days, and Lily halfway considered inquiring about the swim group.

Her current depression had crippled her body so much that she wasn't sure she could walk each Wednesday to swim, but she also knew that she had to do something physical to help herself. Edmund seemed to be surfing all the time now. Any free time he had in his life he devoted to surfing. Lily wanted to find a physical passion in her life too. Noticing Edmund's energy when he would return from surfing made Lily long for that feeling. Losing her mom and then Liana simply drained her of any energy to do anything outside of simple survival, but now she knew she had to make a change, if not just for herself, then for Edmund. And for Liana...

Chapter 18

Iris

Iris chose a cobalt blue suit to wear to work that day. Sometimes the outfit she chose to wear helped her feel stronger. The outfit became like a security blanket. There were times when Iris felt that the more dressed up she was, the less likely her tears would come, but that didn't always work. The large sunglasses were handy and functioned as her Plan B! Iris felt sad at times in her job at the *San Francisco Chronicle* and wished that someone, anyone, would please ask about Cora. Even though she was gone, Iris never wanted to stop talking about her to other people. Just because she only had two and a half years on earth didn't mean that her life didn't matter, or that Iris should forget about her. Cora was her first thought every morning when she would wake up. Why wouldn't anyone ask about her? There were photos all over her desk of all three of her children, but people only asked about the older two. This made Iris feel as though the world was erasing Cora and that just wasn't fair!

Once again, the Monday morning tears started to well up in her eyes and soon Iris was sobbing. Her friends had started to avoid her when she was crying. Iris felt quite certain that the other journalists in her department were whispering about her every time she entered the room. The only time people felt comfortable around her was when she was talking about her current articles on the murals being painted on the walls in the Mission District. Then she seemed very happy and energetic. The message Iris soon began to detect was that unless she avoided talking about Cora, nobody wanted to be close to her. Another reason to feel that persistent pain deep inside of her. Once she was engulfed by the pain in her heart, her old friend, Guilt, would creep into her mind.

Iris recalled a conversation she'd had with Herman during one of Cora's many hospitalizations. They were in what seemed to be a stainless-steel cafeteria on the second floor.

"Iris, a friend of mine was telling me about a hospital in Boston that is doing experimental treatments on children with leukemia." Herman said with hesitance. "What do you think about giving them a call?"

"No! Absolutely not! We are in perfect hands here and my daughter is not going to be experimented on!" Iris screamed at him. She had then stormed out of the cafeteria and hadn't spoken to Herman for days.

This blow-up only caused more guilt for Iris. She had always felt comfortable and trusting of her daughter's doctors, but the thoughts would haunt her that maybe there had been something else out there that they did not explore.

Then she would recall the time when she noticed a slight problem with Cora's eye that even Herman hadn't noticed. The doctors told her it was nothing, that Cora was tired. Iris knew her daughter better and it was later discovered that the leukemia had spread and was affecting her eye.

Am I a crazy person? she would ask herself. Iris desperately wanted her old life back, where she and Herman and their three kids could just pack up and go on a vacation and be happy again. Instead, it had been another afternoon of that feeling that her life was spiraling out of control again. She had to do something to create stability and strength within herself, but what could that be? Iris decided that maybe some routine in her life would help stabilize her. On her way home, she would stop at Sanchez Bath House and inquire about the All-Women's Swim Group.

Chapter 19

Rose & Iris

The little brass bell on Theresa's Flower Shop door rang loudly that morning as Rose entered the shop. She was twenty minutes early to pick up the bouquet of roses for Jacob's grave. Candace was rushing around, still getting things ready for Vivi to cover for her in the flower shop today while she ran the Swim Group. Despite the fact that she was convinced nobody would show up, she still planned on trying to start a group today.

Theresa was still unwilling to come to work today, Vivi had agreed to help out in the flower shop. And of course, Silas and Sophie would also be there to help. When Candace glanced at the sign-up sheet, she discovered that the only person who had actually signed up for the class was Iris Gabriel. She was the tall woman with a large hat and sunglasses who had been in last week. She had told Candace that she swam as a child, but could use some proper lessons and needed the exercise.

The moment Candace saw Rose, she remembered the June red roses she was supposed to have ready that morning! *Oh no! How could I have forgotten?* she thought to herself.

"Hello Rose, so nice to see you!" she practically screamed to Rose. And of course, she had a gentle hug for her. "Oh Rosita, I am so sorry, but I don't have your order ready and I need to run off to teach a swim class. If you'd like, my sister Vivien can prepare the bouquet, but it will take a bit. Would you like a cup of lavender tea while you wait?"

Rose hesitated, as she really wanted Candace to prepare Jacob's bouquet, not her sister! She remembered hearing Candace mention the All-Women's Swim Class and quickly spurted out, "Oh that's no problem. I'm actually here early to tell you that I planned to go to your swim class first and then I'll pick up the bouquet later."

This shocked everyone in the room, including herself! *Oh no, what have I committed to?* she thought in her head. She suddenly realized how important it was for Candace to prepare the bouquet, and not anyone else, as she had done such a perfect job last time. It was as though Rose could actually feel the love Candace had put into her work. *Oh well,* she thought. *I guess I'll be attending a swim class today after all.*

"My second student! Follow me and I will show you around."

As the two of them approached the side entrance to the small pool room they spotted a tall woman wearing rather large, fashionable sunglasses and a big straw hat. "Are you here for the 9:00 Swim Class?" asked Candace.

"Yes, I suppose I am," replied Iris Gabriel in a somewhat sarcastic tone.

"That's wonderful! I'm Candace, the instructor, and this is Rose, our other participant. Let's go on in and I'll take you both to the dressing rooms. We will provide you with swim attire and towels each week. Here's a short questionnaire that I would like for you to complete and then we can get started." Candace explained.

It suddenly became painfully awkward for Rose. In silence, she thought about how when she had left the house this morning, she had no intentions of joining a woman's swim class. Iris Gabriel, on the other hand, was on a mission. She was determined to find something in her life to create stability and perhaps even guidance. Very often in her life she "gave it her all," as her sister would say. "Iris is as strong as an ox!" But deep inside her shredded heart she didn't feel determined or strong at all. She too, in a disguised kind of way, felt as painfully awkward as Rose. No one would ever guess that Iris Gabriel, the Chief Local Events Editor for the *San Francisco Chronicle* was actually very comfortably introverted.

Chapter 20

Sunny

Bright yellow sunflowers always made Sunny smile whether she was in the mood or not. She always managed to smile through her tears when she saw sunflowers. They reminded her of Brandon. Busy Bee sunflowers were his favorite when he was little. He too, used to smile when he would see them. Her sister-in-law, Lizzie, knew this and convinced Sunny that they could stop and pick up some Busy Bees up at the cute flower shop inside the Sanchez Bath House. Even though Sunny hadn't committed to attending the swim group at the bathhouse, Lizzie's secret plan was to get Sunny to the Woman's Swim Class that morning.

The little brass bell rang out again at the flower shop and commanded seven-year-old Silas's attention.

"Good morning, ladies, how can I help you?" the young worker asked as he appeared from behind a large bucket of fresh sunflowers. He was wearing his favorite cap that his grandfather, Ino had given to him. Silas claimed it brought him good luck. His grandmother, Theresa, had embroidered a small patch on the inside of it. In very tiny blue thread it said, "The Pride of San Francisco." She had prepared it and sewn it to the inside of the cap to remind Silas how proud they were of their youngest grandson and how much they loved him. Theresa was always doing special things for her grandchildren. She adored them. It brought her great sadness that Inocencio wasn't by her side anymore to enjoy their family. Watching how happy Ino was when he was with his grandchildren was one of Theresa's favorite things in life. Her heart was crushed at the thought of never again feeling that joy together with Ino.

Silas walked slowly over to the two women. Sunny couldn't help but think of Brandon when he was seven years old. He too, loved wearing caps. Lizzie spoke up and asked if he had information on the swim class that was to start soon.

"Yes, of course, my mom is planning on starting the class in about ten minutes! If you'd like, I can ask my sister, Sophie, to take you to the pool!" he blurted out. Just then, his Auntie Vivien came in and greeted the anxious women.

"Hello ladies. Yes, I can have my niece walk you over to the pool if you would like." Vivien proudly stated. Sunny held her breath for a minute and then decided that since Silas reminded her of Brandon, and since he was tending to the Busy Bee sunflowers when they walked in, that this was a sign that she should definitely participate in the group. Lizzie could tell that Sunny would be in good hands.

"Why don't I run over to my class at the First Cake Bakery on Geary Street and then I'll be back for you in a while?" said Lizzie.

"Yes, yes, that would work," said Sunny cautiously. "But don't be late Lizzie, please." She had to work hard on building the confidence that she needed to survive without Lizzie or Janine at her side. It seemed as though Brandon's death had robbed her of every ounce of the confidence that she once had an overabundance of.

Chapter 21

Lily

The San Francisco fog was slowly dissipating before Lily's eyes. You could almost plan on it every morning at this time of the year. Lily and Edmund both enjoyed the way it made them feel somewhat protected and hidden; feelings they were comfortable with these days. As Lily found a path to the back entrance of the Sanchez Bath House, she observed a beautiful little girl and a woman walking towards her.

"Good morning," said the little brown-haired girl sweetly. "We're on our way to the small pool where my mom is going to teach a swim class to just girls! No boys allowed!" she said confidently. Lily was surprised and took this as a good sign that she wasn't lost or late.

"That's just where I was headed," she said, even though she was rather unsure of herself inside. It was hard for Lily to trust anyone. She had struggled with trust all of her life. Normally, she would have made some excuse as to why she couldn't go with them to the pool, but there was a sort of powerful shifting going on in her heart. As soon as the woman smiled, Lily knew this group might be the one for her. She instantly decided that she would trust the little girl and the woman with the kind smile and followed them just a she had suggested. For about five seconds after she saw the little girl and the woman walking, she envisioned her mom with Liana. It brought an amazing peace to her heart. They would have been so perfect together, she thought as she reminisced on her previous dreams for the future. Perhaps they are together now.

Candace, Rose and Iris were already inside when Lily and Sunny walked in. Candace couldn't believe that four women had fortuitously shown up for her first class! Two weeks ago, she was so sure that no one would come that she'd had no idea what to do about it!

"Well, this is wonderful ladies! Why don't we sit here by the pool and introduce ourselves and maybe talk about what we want this class to be like," she said in a somewhat hesitant voice.

A difficult silence found its way into the room. It was very obvious that this was not going to be a chatty kind of woman's group. It was as though the unbearable sadness in every heart in the room was about to erupt. Candace was not at all prepared for this, but she could see it in all of their eyes; deep shadows of sorrow. Then, suddenly and without realizing it, her daughter Sophie saved the day! She ran into the pool room and shouted, "Mommy, Mommy, you forgot your egg white that Auntie Vivien brought you this morning!"

"Oh my! I'm so sorry ladies," Candace said as she shook her head.

Sophie promptly handed her a small bowl with a cooked egg white in it. "Auntie Vivien already ate the disgusting yolk and she sent this to you!"

The difficult silence in the room transformed into genuine laughter from all of the women.

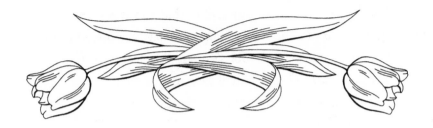

Chapter 22

The large house at 2205 Milton Street was particularly quiet that morning as Theresa pulled her grey sweater closer to herself in order bear the cool fall breeze that was taking up residence in the neighborhood. For about ten years now, each time the autumn season approached, Theresa had strong thoughts that it could be her last, but never had she dreamed that the previous year would be her husband's last autumn on earth.

Theresa moved silently about the house. Mornings were particularly difficult for her. She had always preferred the quiet times in life, but now it was as though she longed for noise. The quiet, especially in Ino's library upstairs, just seemed, in a very blatant way, to make her miss Inocencio even more. It just seemed so impossible that Ino was gone! Despite her unwillingness to go to the flower shop that day, she forced herself to go into her kitchen and prepare some rice pudding for when the kids would arrive later that day. The girls had already planned to bring dinner to their mother's house around 6:00 p.m., so she had plenty of time. Time. Something she wished that she had less of. The days seemed to drag on, but strangely, the weeks were passing by.

It took great determination to rip the October page off her calendar in the kitchen. It seemed to represent that rude way that life really does go on. She held on tightly to the months as they went by. She had already waited several days before she could change the month. A new month without him, she thought as she wiped away her tears with her apron. Just as the seasons of the year triggered changes in the leaves on the trees, so did the calendar and certain dates trigger unique pains in Theresa's soul — pains that were impossible to understand.

Making rice pudding would ease the feelings in her heart and put a smile on her face, as it would be a pleasant reminder of Ino. He had loved her rice pudding when he was alive, and everyone knew that. It brought Theresa joy to think about him.

"Don't forget to put raisins in the pudding, *Querida.*" he would say, despite the fact that she always put raisins in the pudding. Cutting the amount of sugar in half to adjust to Ino's diabetic needs had been a habit, and it continued even though he was no longer there to eat his favorite dessert. Theresa felt Ino's presence through her rice pudding, something she could never have predicted back in the days when he had sat in that old brown chair, while she prepared dinner each evening.

There were so many adjustments to life as a widow that had presented themselves to Theresa. She would adapt to some and ignore others. No matter what the situation was, it always seemed to relate to the loss of

88

her husband, but staying home gave her comfort. It felt as though his soul still resided there and she could hold on to it in a spiritual kind of way. Feeling his presence in her home was something she never talked about to anyone for fear of being hauled off to an insane asylum. Theresa knew she wasn't crazy, yet sometimes that out of place feeling inside of her became very strong.

Where do I belong? Theresa wondered.

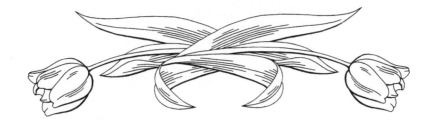

Chapter 23

Candace could physically feel the deep sorrow in each of the ladies faces as they all turned to her for direction once little Sophie left the pool area. Even in the ladies' voices, she could hear the great sadness that they all possessed. It was familiar to her. Maybe it was because she, too, had experienced a great sorrow when her father had died. Her decision for today was to simply have them complete the one-page questionnaire and give them a brief tour of the facility and dressing rooms. Candace informed them that they would be provided with swimsuits, caps, and towels. She explained that previous classes had lasted seven weeks, but that it would be fine if they wanted to continue the class past seven weeks.

The hours seemed acceptable to everyone and for some reason, Wednesday was also a perfect day for all of them.

As the ladies introduced themselves to each other a sense of peace entered the room. Although none of them said it, they were all searching for something in their lives, something that could give them the courage they needed to continue moving forward. Each of them longed desperately for the past as their children continued to nudge at their thoughts. Yet they each knew that the past was gone and impossible to relive. The future also seemed impossible because it didn't have Jacob, Liana, Brandon, or Cora in it.

****

Later that evening at Theresa's house, after enjoying a wonderful meal, Candace and Vivien reviewed the questionnaires only to discover that all of the ladies' names were names of flowers!

"What a lovely coincidence!" said Vivien.

"No auntie Vivi, it's a sign," said Silas.

"No auntie Vivi, it's a sign," echoed Sophie.

Theresa smiled. She had always believed in signs, and longed to connect with Inocencio if only he would send her one. There was no doubt in her mind that he was watching over all of them. That's what kept her going on hard days like today.

Chapter 24

Rose & Iris

Once again, Rose arrived twenty minutes early for the swim class on Wednesday. She was usually late to most of her commitments these days, but strangely enough, she woke up bright and early that morning because she wanted to have plenty of time to stop by her parents' home prior to class and still arrive early.

"Good morning, Dad!" Rose shouted as she entered their home through the kitchen. "Good morning, Mom!" She walked down the hallway towards her mother's bedroom.

"Rosita, could you please look for the *Borrowed Angel* book today?" asked her mother. Rose rolled her eyes as she tried for a minute to pretend not to hear her mother's request from down the hall.

"Yes, Mom. I will look," she replied. Rose's elderly parents were always happy to see her, but they also had many needs that only she could fulfill. They had started keeping a list on a tablet so that they would not forget to ask her. Rose's mom, Carmelita, had been searching for a book entitled *Borrowed Angel* for many years. She claimed she had read it as a child. The book had been a gift from her mother, whose best friend, Marguerite Hamilton, was the author. She was originally from San Francisco. When they had tried contacting her for a copy, they were sad to hear that she had died years before. Still, Carmelita was determined and had faith that Rose would find a copy of the book. It had become an obsession for her. She had secretly decided that Rose needed something to get her out of the house after Jacob died. Rose had been so involved in caring for him that his death had created a huge void in her life. Perhaps searching for *Borrowed Angel* would give her something to do. Carmelita had been diagnosed with cancer recently and Rose was not about to argue with her.

"I'll stop by Mission Lights Bookstore on my way home today," Rose added. Guilt was a great motivator, and Rose's mom knew how to push that button! "I have to go now. I'll see you tomorrow."

****

Iris was also early for swim class that morning. She was often early for her appointments.

"Hello, um... Rose, is it?," Iris asked.

"Yes, yes," said Rose, "And you are Iris, correct?"

"Yes, I'm Iris."

At first, the two of them just looked at their feet and then simultaneously started talking, which then made it more uncomfortable because they couldn't understand what each other had said. Then, suddenly, Rose surprised herself by saying, "Iris Gabriel, the author of *Lessons From a*

Gentle Life? I loved that book! I read it recently. My son died — Well, yes, my— my son died."

Now the tears welled up in both of their eyes. There was instantly an unforeseen mutual respect that implanted itself in their broken hearts.

"May I ask? How did you hear about my book?" asked Iris.

"Well, I've been on this mission to find a book for my mother, so I've been searching everywhere, and I came across *Lessons From a Gentle Life*. I read it cover to cover in one night! It is beautiful. The book I'm looking for was a gift from my grandmother to my mother when she was little. She wants to find it so that she can read it before..." Rose paused and held her breath. "My mother was diagnosed with kidney cancer. About a month ago she was in a small car accident that left her very sore afterwards. Pretty soon the soreness got worse, and here we are now watching her slowly die of cancer."

Rose couldn't believe that she had just said that out loud! It had been very difficult to accept her mother's diagnosis and she had told very few people. It was somehow easy for her to talk with Iris. Maybe it was because reading her book had helped her get to know her before they had even met.

"*Borrowed Angel* is about a mother and her daughter, who eventually dies. She says it's really about their beautiful relationship. I haven't been able to find it, but I did find your book and loved it! I must say, it is the most accurate book on love and loss of a child that I have ever read," continued Rose. "I'm sure your book has helped many people."

"Thank you, Rose. I appreciate that," whispered Iris. "You might try looking for *Borrowed Angel* at the People's Library downtown. They have lots of hard to find books there".

"Thanks Iris, I will," said Rose.

This gave Rose another purpose. She wanted to find the rare book before it was too late. Her mother's eyesight was starting to fail, just like everything else in her weak body. After caring for Jacob, she had become all too familiar with the signs that someone was slowly saying goodbye. Her mother was sleeping more and more these days, she had noticed. How could this be happening again? *I can't do this,* Rose often repeated in her head. *I just can't lose another person in my life. It's too much for one human to endure.*

Chapter 25

The ordinary echoing sound inside pool areas was absent in the pool room that morning as the ladies gathered. Candace thought that was strange, and wondered why. It sounded as though they were outside in the ocean. It distracted her at first, and then she just let it go. *Maybe it's because everyone here is so soft spoken,* she thought. *Or, maybe there is something special about this pool.*

The ladies seemed quite comfortable with each other. They moved about the pool, enjoying the water. It was warm and felt great. Rose immediately relaxed and smiled to herself. It was kind of like a bath at home. Very peaceful. Lily felt calmer than she had been in months simply enjoying the seawater. Sunny felt safe, and that was rare for her. Iris knew immediately that the decision to come here today was the right one.

"Today we will practice floating," said Candace in a kind and confident voice. "Feel free to find a space and simply float. You can close your eyes if you want."

Feeling weightless was a simple, yet much needed pleasure that all of them enjoyed. It felt very relaxing to all of the ladies. It was just what they needed. There was definitely a sense of trust that was present in the pool with them. The ambience in the pool room was something Sunny had never felt before. It was safe and peaceful. At one point, Iris felt as though she might fall asleep while she was floating. Even though floating around in the pool did not engage the women as a group activity would have, they all seemed connected. It was as though the water had the ability to comfort each of them individually and simultaneously. Perhaps the weightless feeling they all experienced helped them leave the heavy feelings of grief and guilt behind.

This is just what my mother needs, thought Candace to herself. *If only I could convince her to join the group.*

Later that evening, Vivien asked Candace what the class did that day. Candace giggled and said, "Well, we floated and then... we floated! A peaceful day of just letting go. It was wonderful!"

"You just had them float? That's it? You didn't teach them anything? Just floating? That's interesting," said Vivien.

"Oh, Vivi, you are such a teacher! I want this to be more of a group than a class. I want the ladies to do whatever they want," said Candace. "It's not as though I have to follow lesson plans for this."

"Well, remind me never to be a sub in that class!" Vivien shouted gleefully.

"The Art of Floating, the secret to a successful life," said Candace as they both laughed out loud.

Vivien had recently started a part-time job as a school librarian with the San Francisco School System, but expenses were rising, and she was going to need a second job to help supplement their expenses. *Hmm,* she thought, *Working two jobs might mean that I might have to come to Candace's class just to float away the stress!*

Chapter 26

Rose & Iris: After Swim Class

After class, Iris and Rose were discussing a plan to meet at the People's Library later that day.

"I know a young man who can find any book you are looking for. This guy is amazing! He can surely locate *Borrowed Angel* for your mother," offered Iris.

"Oh no, I just remembered that I have band practice later today. We have a performance at Jazz at JuJu's this weekend and I am not ready at all!" exclaimed Rose. "Can we plan for next week?"

"Well... yes, I guess that will be fine," said Iris, but in her mind, she knew that she would be going to the People's Library this afternoon. It had always been difficult for Iris to put things off for another time, especially when it involved finding a special book for someone who may not have a lot of time left on earth.

Holding Cora in her arms for the last time, had taught Iris the meaning of 'sacred moments.' Recalling her precious time with Cora was a gift. She had learned not to put things off for another time because that time may never come.

****

Lessons From a Gentle Life was still beautifully displayed in the entrance of the library. Iris loved seeing the book, as it had Cora sitting at her piano on the cover. A special nurse who had cared for Cora in the hospital had painted a watercolor for Iris and Herman during her treatment. It was beautiful, and Iris chose it for the book cover.

"Hello, Mark Fite! How are you doing?" she whispered to the young man behind the desk.

"Well, Miss Iris Gabriel, what a treat to see you today," said Mark. He stood up immediately and reached over to give Iris a gentle hug. "How can I be of assistance to you?"

"Well, I'm here in search of a rare book. The title is *Borrowed Angel* and a friend of mine is trying to find it for her mother. The author is Marguerite Hamilton."

"Hmm," said Mark, "that name sounds familiar. Give me a little time."

While Mark looked for the book, Iris wandered around the library. As a journalist and a professional author, it was comforting to be surrounded by the written word. Iris had always loved books and writing. They brought joy to her heart in a familiar way. "Books heal loneliness," she would say.

After Cora died, Iris wanted desperately to document her short life. It was a powerful one, as so many people were touched by Cora. People that Iris and Herman didn't even know would reach out to them and comment on their amazing daughter and what she had done for them. This comforted both of them, but Iris had wanted it to last forever. She was determined to stay dedicated to what little Cora had been trying to tell the world!

****

Mark startled Iris with his excited squeal when he approached her a short time later. "Not only did I find *Borrowed Angel* for you, Miss Iris, but I found the first book Marguerite Hamilton wrote! It's called *Red Shoes for Nancy*. It turns out that *Borrowed Angel* is the sequel!"

"Oh my, I wonder if Rose is even aware of the first book. I'll take them both! Thank you so much, Mark. I knew you would be able to help," said Iris as she smiled in a flirtatious way.

Iris held on tight to both books as she made her way back home. She arrived in time for Herman to drop off their children. She even had enough time to skim through the books, as she was a little curious of their content. Finding these treasures for Rose was very satisfying for Iris, and she sensed that Rose needed to create precious memories with her dying mother.

Iris knew all too well what it was like to have a mother in her last decade of life and wanted to help. She felt inspired to call her own mother in Chicago that evening to check on her.

"Hello, Mom? It's Iris. How are you doing?"

"Oh, I'm fine and dandy like a piece of candy Iris, how are you and the kids?" her mom said jokingly. She was aging and lonely, and Iris could sense it. Her mother was one of the people in her life that she really trusted and wanted to be like. Iris remembered that the *San Francisco Chronicle* had recently asked her to work on a story about the railroad.

It would involve her traveling back to Chicago again. That night Iris and her mother planned for her to bring the kids along and they could spend more time visiting with her sister and their cousins. Herman would surely support her decision, she could count on that. He believed in family and had always had great respect for her mother.

Chapter 27

Lily Gets Brave

Once again, upon entering the pool room for her class, Candace felt the absence of the echo sound in the room. *This is really strange,* she thought, *but I like it.* She wondered if anyone else had noticed. *It softens the noise in here when class starts, and it definitely facilitates the calm atmosphere in the room and allows the women to hear each other's voices clearly. That's something that is not easy to create in a group,* Candace decided. She thought of it as a sacred silence that could promote listening. That, in addition to the weightless feeling they all got when in the water, made it seem like some sort of healing was beginning for the swim group.

Lily was having a hard morning that Wednesday, and the other women immediately recognized that something was wrong. In each of their own supporting ways, they all tried to make Lily feel better.

The night before, Lily had decided that she would tell the group that she was pregnant. She was determined to bring it up because at the rate her tummy was growing, very soon the question might come up and she wanted to be pro-active with the discussion. Her clothes no longer fit her, and that was triggering many emotions connected to her pregnancy with Liana.

Her halfwit sister-in-law had recently suggested that she simply pretend this was her first baby in order to avoid talking about Liana, but that didn't go over very well with Lily or Edmund.

"I don't know what to do!" she screamed to Edmund. "Someone is going to ask if this is my first baby and I don't know if I can talk about Liana yet, and I'm certainly not going to tell them that this is my first pregnancy, because it's not!"

Lily loved her swim class and decided that she could trust the women there, and so would tell them Liana's story today!

She began by telling the group about her first loss. Her mother, Susan.

"My mother was like a friend to me. She always knew just what to say to make me feel better. Then she got a brain tumor and stopped talking altogether," Lily shared in her bravest voice. "That was a loss in itself, but then she died before my baby, Liana, was even born."

The group listened respectfully to every word Lily said. It was probably the hardest thing she had ever done. That devastating Christmas when Liana died would always remain as the worst day in Lily's life, and now she was talking about it out loud. She felt as though the more she spoke the lighter the burden of her loss felt. The women in the group seemed to feel her pain and this felt very therapeutic for Lily.

****

Sunny could totally relate to Lily's mixed emotions around the Christmas Holiday as she, too, had experienced a great loss at the same time of the year. Sunny felt a powerful sorrow for Lily and listened with intense empathy. She wanted to take her pain away and heal her from any pain she felt. Hearing her tell the group that Liana had died made Sunny realize how grateful she could be for having had Brandon here on earth for twenty-three years.

Everyone listened attentively and with great courage. The amount of bravery within the room was unfathomable. It was so hard to keep from crying as Lily's sweet voice described perfectly her love for her mother Susan and baby Liana. The tears rolled down the ladies' faces and mixed with the salty sea water in the pool. Later that evening, Vivien commented to Candace that the group would surely continue to float with the addition of probably a gallon of salty tears.

Once her story was told, Lily felt a huge relief. She felt a kind of new joy for her second baby.

The night after she had told the group about her mother and Liana, she was able to think about names for their baby, which was something she and Edmund had completely avoided until now. This made her feel very excited about her pregnancy.

****

Edmund continued to stay busy, both at work and at the beach. He was determined to erase his own sorrow over losing Liana. He just didn't know how. He wanted to support Lily, but also felt weak at times. One day at the beach, something happened that gave him some inner strength and confidence. He was surfing in a place he was not very familiar with.

Suddenly, some strange sounds came his way. There was shouting and splashing and lots of chaos coming from behind him.

"Help! Help! I'm drowning!" someone screamed a panic voice.

"Please, come quick! I can't hold him anymore!" screamed another voice.

Edmunds heart began to beat faster. He saw that a boat had capsized in the ocean. Men appeared to be drowning, and he was the only one in sight! With his quick thinking and First Aid skills, he was able to save eight men's lives by making three trips to and from the beach carrying the men on his surf board! Once they were on dry land, Edmund tended to their serious injuries.

By giving the drowning men hope, Edmund found hope. Hope; something that had completely lost its meaning in his life after the death of his daughter. He had so desperately wished he could have saved Liana's life. Accepting the hugs and appreciation from the men whose lives he had saved felt surprisingly wonderful. Edmund couldn't wait to tell Lily all about it.

Chapter 28

Sunny

Danny and Sunny had found themselves crippled when it came to doing things in their lives that, in the past, had brought them great joy. The overwhelming guilt that had been a constant companion for them after Brandon's suicide was affecting them both in a harsh way.

Before their boys were even born, they had purchased a beach house where they spent time during Danny's vacation time. They had created many memories there with the family, but now they both felt that it was unfair that Brandon was not there to share the joys of life, so they simply suppressed any happy feelings or activities, including visiting the beach house. Their three other sons were starting to feel rejected and unimportant. Once this came to Sunny's attention, however, she did everything in her power to change that.

Sunny and Danny adored all of their sons and wanted desperately to pick up the pieces, but there were too many and they were scattered everywhere. It was as though their lives had simply exploded. They felt distant from others at times because they had no explanation as to what happened in Brandon's life to cause him to end it. The grieving parents felt Brandon's pain and had actually became accustomed to it. They felt that they did not deserve to be happy anymore because Brandon was gone.

Danny became consumed in his job at the Bureau. He was often involved in saving lives, but a haunting thought always crept into his mind even when the Department was forever giving him praise. *Why wasn't I there to save my own son's life?* Danny privately and continuously asked himself.

Sunny had to learn how to live all over again. There were days when even getting out of bed took every ounce of energy she possessed. She would eventually drag herself to the coffee pot and then cry her eyes out.

Fortunately, their families were there to check on them and provide the support and love that they needed to survive. One morning, Sunny found a bouquet of sunflowers left by an anonymous, sweet person on their front porch. This was truly an example of the love her family felt for her and Danny.

And of course, spending time with Brandon's son Luke was life-saving! Sunny was determined to keep Brandon's story alive. She held on to favorite memories and always talked about her son.

Her biggest fear was that he would be forgotten by everyone, including his own family. This fear actually created a positive energy inside of her that, in turn, gave her strength. The strength they all prayed for. Any time Sunny had the opportunity, she told a "Brandon story." Like the time when he was very young and had memorized a children's book when he was in kindergarten. He read it out loud to the entire class as though he could already read. This always brought a proud smile to her face.

They soon got involved in a group to help young people who were battling with thoughts of suicide. As a family, they participated in spreading awareness about the complicated problem that so many young people live with. Hiding or ignoring the problem wasn't going to help, and the Andersons knew that.

After the day that Lily told the group about Liana, and that she was pregnant again, Sunny felt as though maybe she could also trust the group and planned to tell them how Brandon had died. She had already hinted that she had lost a son, but never really talked about how he had died. As Lily described the helpless feeling of losing Liana, Sunny could totally relate. It was such an impossible feeling. It didn't make any sense. How could they be such competent mothers and still lose their children to death? How in the world could this happen? Sunny had always felt so confident and capable. Not anymore.

Chapter 29

Iris

Iris had checked her watch four times in the last two minutes as she stood nervously outside the train station in Oakland. Herman had promised to bring Erin and Vanessa, packed and ready, for their trip to visit their grandmother in Chicago, while she worked on the story for the San Francisco Chronicle.

That morning was particularly difficult because packing only for herself had felt so strange. There weren't the usual decisions on what to pack or not pack for Cora. She cried when she walked out the door with only one small bag for herself. She would have carried ten bags if it meant that Cora could be on the trip with them. That feeling that she was always forgetting something or leaving someone behind never left her. That someone was Cora.

Iris would be missing several Wednesday swim classes, but she had thoughtfully dropped off the two books that she had checked out of the library for Rose. She had located Candace at the flower shop and trusted her to give them to Rose that week. She carefully wrote a note to Rose explaining that Mark Fite had found the first book, *Red Shoes for Nancy*, that *Borrowed Angel* was the sequel to. She found out later that Rose's eyes filled with tears when Candace gave her the books and she read the note. Never before in her life had Rose felt so grateful to a friend. She couldn't wait to see Iris again to properly thank her.

"Mom, we made it!" screamed Vanessa. Time to focus, Iris told herself. She wanted this trip to be special for the kids. There were so many miles between them and her mother. After the divorce, Iris had entertained the idea of moving back there, but that wouldn't have been fair to Herman and the kids. It would have destroyed them, and Cora's death had already hurt all of them so deeply that she quickly dismissed that option. Fortunately, they had this opportunity to visit and spend quality time with her mother this week. She gently closed her eyes and took herself back in time to when she was a little girl, happily making sugar cookies with her mother in Chicago.

As they boarded the train, Iris's heart skipped a beat. She felt that long lost emotion, excitement, again. It was strange. She really hadn't felt that way since Cora died. It felt good for a minute, but she quickly dismissed it. For now, she would simply enjoy the kids and look forward to seeing her mom and family. She hadn't become comfortable with excitement in her life yet, and wasn't sure she wanted to. It scared her, but she definitely recognized the familiar feeling. You would never know the depths of her sorrow over losing Cora that existed inside her heart. There was always such a disconnect between the outside world and the Iris inside who felt so alone.

Chapter 30

Rose

"Mom! Mom! You are never going to believe this!" shouted Rose as she ran inside her parents' house.

"What Rosita? What on earth is going on?" answered Carmelita's her soft, frail voice from her bedroom.

"Was there an earthquake?" asked her dad as he shuffled his way in from the back room. "What's going on?"

"No, Guppy," Rose said to her dad. She always called him by his nickname when she was excited about something. "Where's Mom? I have a surprise for her!"

"Well, I think she was taking a nap. She's been canning peaches all morning in the shed," said her Dad.

"Canning peaches? Are you kidding? She's too weak for that!" Rose said. She walked into her parents' bedroom and saw that her mom was indeed laying down. "Oh Mom, are you okay? I have a surprise for you! I found the book! *Borrowed Angel*! Look! And here's another book that Marguerite Hamilton wrote before it!"

Carmelita sat up slowly and smiled. Both women hugged and then each hastily wiped tears from her eyes before the other noticed.

"I have a friend from my swim class who is a writer herself, and she was able to locate both books for us!" Carmelita could no longer hide her tears.

"Oh Rosita, this is the best news I've heard in all my life!" said her mom.

"Oh Mom, please," said Rose as she rolled her eyes. What Carmelita really wanted to say was that this was the happiest that she had seen Rose since Jacob died, and it really touched her to see her daughter so happy again. She worried constantly about her. So did Rose's dad, Eduardo, or 'Guppy,' as the grandchildren had nicknamed him. Carmelita and Eduardo adored Rose and were deeply saddened when Jacob died. There were times when they felt more hurt about what his death had done to their daughter, than what they felt about losing their grandson. Theirs was a double grief as they mourned for both Jacob and for Rose. Then, when Carmelita was diagnosed with cancer, they were both terrified to tell her the news. It seemed impossible for one family to have so many tragedies! They couldn't imagine feeling any more pain or loss.

Later that evening, Rose decided that the next weekend she would start reading the book aloud to her mother. Carmelita's eyes were very weak, and it would be fun to read to her. They often experienced uncomfortable silences when they were together, and reading would create a special bond between them. She would be forever grateful to Iris for finding the books that would help create precious memories for her and her family. This is truly a miracle, Rose thought to herself. She was so happy that she had joined the swim group!

Meanwhile, Iris was on the train with her children on her way to create her own precious memories with her mother in Chicago, thanks to Rose for inspiring her.

Chapter 31

Sunny

Sunny usually started off her day by picking up after their dog, who was forever making messes in the backyard. That morning, she was particularly sad, as it was the day after Brandon's birthday. She wandered off to the rocky left side of the house, where she rarely went. It was as though a voice inside her called her over for a sweet surprise. There it stood, all alone but tall and proud; a single sunflower, shining with the most beautiful yellow color that seemed to match Luke's golden curls. Sunny stood still, graciously accepting it for all of its beauty and glory. Tears came to her eyes as she felt Brandon's presence in his favorite flower. Her love for him could never die, and continued to grow as, at that moment, she was beginning to let go of all the guilt she had held inside.

Sunny could hardly contain herself as she went back indoors, anxious to tell Danny about the sunflower on the side of the house.

"Danny! Danny! Where are you? You have to come and see what I just found!" she shouted in her old strong and confident voice.

"What's up Sunny? Are you alright?" Danny asked. As he made his way towards Sunny, there was something different about him that Sunny noticed immediately. He was looking deeply into her eyes. They both suddenly felt differently and were not at all uncomfortable facing each other as if for the first time. After Brandon's suicide, a monstrous sense of guilt had prevented them from truly facing each other. They both felt it and avoided it at all costs. Guilt has a way of isolating people and creating distance between them. But for some reason, today was different. Danny and Sunny had simultaneously let go of the guilt they both carried and became closer than they had ever been in their relationship. They looked into each other's eyes and gently hugged each other before walking outside together to enjoy Brandon's sunflower.

Danny had saved so many people in different ways through his job with the Bureau, but he had a hard time feeling proud of that. What he really wanted to do was to go back in time and save his son's life. It was too late for that, and that hurt Danny in the cruelest way. It was time to let that go or it would interfere with his relationships with his wife, his other sons, and his grandson. The sunflower helped Danny move forward. It was time.

There were many things about Brandon that they did not understand while he was alive, but those things were starting to fade. We never really completely understand our children and their decisions in life, but we never stop loving them. We may have a hard time accepting them, but we never stop loving them. Both Sunny and Danny believed this, but it took a long time to be strong in this belief. It disappeared from their hearts at times and caused them great sadness, but with support from others and special signs from heaven, they always came back to the realization that they never stopped loving Brandon. He was always in both their hearts. That love was precious and now they could share it with his son, Luke.

Later that morning, Sunny decided to share with the swim group about how Brandon had taken his life. This step was huge for her, but she felt safe with these women and she could trust that they would never judge her or blame her. After all, they had all experienced losing a child and certainly understood that painful loss.

"Candace, is it alright if I share with the group something about my son, Brandon?" Sunny said quietly.

Candace had been waiting for this moment.

"We have been meeting together for a while now and you know you can trust us," Candace responded.

Sunny began, "Brandon was always a quiet son. He loved to pray and often talked about angels when he was little. I suppose he had his fears, but he never talked about them. Both Danny and I had no idea how depressed he had become during the time he was on the ship. He was the chef, and I imagine he spent lots of time by himself. I suppose we will never know what caused him to take his life, and maybe it really doesn't matter."

"What does matter is that we never forget him and what he meant to all of us. His gentle manner, his curly brown hair, his sense of humor and his peaceful way. I have all of his pictures and some letters that I will share with his little boy when he is old enough."

The women all listened with empathetic hearts. They silently communicated their respect for Sunny and allowed her to talk about the most difficult thing that had ever happened to her.

At one point or another, it seemed as though they all had felt guilty about something relating to their individual losses. Iris had mentioned once that it was because of their roles as parents that they felt they should be able to control everything that went on with their children, including death. She had shared with the group that when Cora died of leukemia, all of that control went out the window and left her powerless and completely helpless. All of the women agreed and could relate to that feeling.

"We will never understand why Brandon chose to end his life, but we do feel he didn't end his love for us or his son," Sunny continued softly. "That love is forever, and we share it with his son Luke every time we remind him of the gentle, loving way Brandon would hold him when he was an infant."

After class, each of the women went out of their way to give Sunny gentle hugs in the warm waiting area outside the pool. She accepted those embraces and cherished those moments. Her life had slowed down since Brandon's death. She didn't rush through life anymore. She was glad that she had shared Brandon's story with the group and easily accepted each of their sincere hugs. Danny used to tease her that she had become an expert "hug analyzer." She learned from this experience the difference between a sincere hug and a fake hug. Today there were only sincere hugs.

Sunny could hardly wait to get home to that tall, glorious sunflower she had discovered that morning. *What a gift!* she thought to herself.

Chapter 32

Iris

The Chicago winds were finally calming down after a long, sleepless night at Iris' childhood home. Saying goodbye to her mother after what felt like the best time of her life was feeling like an impossible task. As Iris and her mother held on to each other tightly in the kitchen, tears poured from their eyes.

"Oh Mom, I wish I could put you in my pocket and take you back to San Francisco with me!" That made Iris' mom laugh out loud, and then the two of them were able to let each other go.

"Well, you can't do that, so you will just have to plan another trip soon my dear. Now, here are some treats for you and the children for your journey on the train," said her mom as she handed her a tin of homemade cookies. Iris and her mother had always enjoyed making cookies together and now that tradition was continuing with Vanessa and Erin. The night before, the four of them must have made a hundred cookies!

"I promise we will be back soon Mom," said Iris closing her eyes. The kids watched both of them and smiled when they heard that they may be returning soon. Spending time in Chicago always lifted Iris' spirits, and when she was happy, they were very happy.

"I'm hosting my church group meeting at my house next week and I have lots of cleaning to do to prepare," Iris announced, changing the subject.

"Oh Iris, that sounds great! I'm sure your friends enjoy that," said her mom. She worried about Iris, especially since the divorce. Iris had always been a hard worker and seldom took time out for herself. Her mom recalled a memory of Iris as a child helping her hang out laundry on the clothes line in the summer months. She was forever wanting to help.

The clackety train ride back to the West Coast was long and hard, but Iris did need to get back home to San Francisco. The train would take them to Oakland and then they would need to catch a ferry to California Street in San Francisco.

The New Hope church group that she belonged to was always changing. People came and went all the time. It seemed as though people would come to a few meetings and then stop. Iris searched for consistency and continuity in her life and maybe that was why she really liked her swim class. She had never belonged to another group that had such perfect attendance! Rose, Sunny and Lily all reminded her of a close supporting friend from the past. Her name was Agnes and would have fit in perfectly with the swim class.

The year Cora was diagnosed with leukemia, Iris met Agnes, who she had managed to keep in touch with over the years. She and her husband

126

had moved to Portland to care for Agnes' aging mother. Her father had died years earlier of the Spanish Flu, and her mother was alone. In the 1920s, the Spanish Flu poured out grief by the gallons as it took thousands of lives, including the lives of many of Agnes' relatives. When Cora died, Iris' friend came back to San Francisco for the funeral. She had promised Iris that she would be there for her, and she was. They were there for each other. Despite living in different states, they wrote to each other monthly and shared many things about their lives. Agnes' mother died a few years later, and Iris was able to console her in a beautiful and genuine way. The two of them always kept in touch and exchanged gifts on each other's birthdays and at Christmas time. They had started off giving each other coffee mugs, but they were both starting to have quite the collection, so they switched to kitchen towels and books. That idea was perfect because they always needed them, and they were easier to store and mail!

Friendship was highly important to Iris as it helped ease her grief. She could always count on Agnes and felt comfortable talking about her loss to her. It was like a gift to her to have a friend who knew her daughter and remembered her well. Herman and the kids didn't mention Cora unless Iris brought her up. She figured they were afraid they might upset her, but the truth was, she thought about Cora all the time.

Chapter 33

Candace and Vivien had decided to meet in North Beach to do a little shopping for Vivien's oldest son's birthday present. May was coming up soon and they wanted to get Patrick something special. Their plans were to get him several small gifts, put them all together in a box, and make it from the entire family. Patrick was turning 13 and wasn't easy to shop for.

Vivi was great at gift giving. She always had amazing, unique ideas, and usually included a book when it came to gifts. "I wish I had a job giving gifts," she said to Candace as their trolley car stopped with a long screech.

"Yes, as second job, it would be a perfect way to supplement your salary at the school library, Vivi. And you could do it on your own time!" said Candace.

"Maybe someday I could open up my own business, 'Care Packages by Vivien,' Vivien mused. She had always been very good at cheering people up when they were down. Her gifts and cards were magical and always so personal. She spent lots of time thinking about what was important to different people and what might make them smile. It really upset her to see people sad. She would cry silently.

People often commented that they received her gifts on days that they really needed them. Timing was a special talent that seemed to come naturally to her without her even knowing it. But today they were shopping for Patrick's upcoming birthday and the pressure was on!

"How about a yo-yo, Vivi?" asked Candace as they strolled through Lola's in North Beach.

"A yo-yo? What is that?" asked Vivien.

"Well, it's a small, round wooden toy with a string on it that you make wind up and down with your hand," replied Candace. "Look, here it is." She attempted to demonstrate. But instead of going up and down, the yo-yo flew right out of Candace's hand and rolled to the middle of the store. Candace looked at Vivien in shock. The yo-yo kept rolling and reached the door just as a customer was walking in! Candace gasped and Vivi let out a nervous laugh. The toy seemed to be picking up speed and rolled out the door onto Grant Street. From there, it rolled down the steep hill and into Washington Square Park! Candace immediately chased after the runaway yo-yo and recovered it.

"Oh my, I am so sorry," said Vivien to the shop owner.

"What on earth have you done?" he asked her, annoyed.

"Oh, well we were just shopping for a gift for my son and we wanted to try out the yo-yo and it just yo-yoed out the door! I will pay you for it right now, I promise," she answered nervously as she took out her change purse. The two sisters laughed all the way home as they tried to clean off the marks that the yo-yo had picked up on its adventure through the park.

Later that evening, Vivien read the instructions that came in the yo-yo box and learned that a businessman named Pedro Flores, who was from the Philippines, had been the first person to mass-produce yo-yos at his small toy factory located in Santa Barbara. She found it fascinating that in the native language of the Philippines, the word yo-yo means "come back." *What a perfect gift,* she thought to herself.

Chapter 34

Lily

Edmund had been very quiet at first when Lily arrived home. She knew something was up by the way he just sort of paced around the house straightening out paintings on the walls. Then he offered to fix dinner later that evening. That was good because she was in no mood to cook. She was feeling anxious and fatigued and didn't really understand why. The changes in her body made her feel uncomfortable and she simply couldn't relax.

"Oh Edmund, just come out with it! What do you want to say to me?" Lily snapped at him.

"Oh, well, uh, nothing Lily. I just wondered how your day went," he said nervously.

"It was fine. I'm fine. I had a fine day!" Lily shouted.

Edmund quickly decided not to tell her about how he had saved eight drowning men's lives that morning! He could tell that Lily wasn't feeling well. It just wasn't the time. This pregnancy seemed to be taking a toll on both of them and he was nervous around Lily. So many emotions were always going through both of them. But he was grateful for Lily's swim group and very glad when she had shared with them that she had lost her mother and Liana. He was also relieved when she told him that she had told the group that she was pregnant again.

Later that evening, as the sun began to set and the light in their home was changing, Lily decided to make them both a cup of tea. That was something they had always enjoyed together. Perhaps it was her way of apologizing to Edmund for being so short with him earlier. Her mother had always believed that tea brought peace to the soul.

"A cup of tea always heals any troubles you may be carrying," she would say.

As Lily walked slowly down the hall of their home, trying to avoid the steps that caused the floor to creak loudly, she paused at the closed door to her right. That was Liana's room. Inside, it remained exactly as it had been left the day she died, only now the door was always closed. She turned back to face Edmund and in each other's eyes, they saw the same thing. It was time to go through the many gifts they had received for Liana's baby shower and decide what they would use for the new baby they were soon to have. This created sadness for Lily because it felt as though she was dismissing Liana in a small way.

"Maybe we should put off going through those things until after the baby is born," suggested Edmund.

"Why? Are you afraid this baby will die too?" asked Lily.

"No, no, not at all Lily! I just don't want to put you through any more sadness," answered Edmund.

"Well, I want to go through the gifts and decide what we will give away, what we will use now, and who knows, maybe we can save some of it for our grandchildren!" Lily was surprised by how strong her voice sounded.

"Great, Lily! I would love to do that whenever you are ready, my dear," said Edmund.

So, after their tea that evening, Lily and Edmund bravely and lovingly went through many outfits, blankets, toys, and baby supplies and created three piles. They nicknamed the piles the Past, the Present and the Future. It was definitely a therapeutic way to let go of some of their past dreams and create future dreams together. This task was not without strong emotions and tears, but it brought the two of them together in a glorious way. Later that night, they decided that if this baby was a girl, she would be named Naomi Olivia and if it was a boy, he would be named Matthew.

Lily seemed to be gaining weight slowly in the beginning of her pregnancy, but now in her sixth month, her weight caught up and she felt huge. Edmund thought so too, and wondered why, but in spite of that, Lily's pregnancy was finally feeling more exciting than frightening for both of them. Little did they know, there was a good reason why Lily felt huge.

Several months later, they found themselves in the labor room at the hospital, holding on to each other, with all of the hope in the world for a healthy baby. Three hours later, after Lily had been moved to the delivery room, the doctor casually walked into the small room where Edmond anxiously awaited news.

"Well, what names have you chosen?" asked the doctor.

"Uh, names? You mean like more than one?"

"Yes! Your wife just delivered two healthy baby girls, Edmund. Congratulations!"

Once she was back home, Lily called her father on the telephone.

"Yes, Dad, you have twin granddaughters and they are anxious to meet you!" she said. "I hope you are ready for babysitting duty soon, because I need to get out of this house."

Olivia and Naomi were a handful, and life was busy in their home. Edmund never did tell Lily that he was a hero to eight families and to the entire surfing community. He still wished that he could have been a hero to Liana.

****

One month earlier, Iris had coincidently written a story for the *San Francisco Chronicle* about the local surfer who had saved eight men's lives with his surf board. She had interviewed Edmund and only realized later that he was Lily's husband.

"When I asked Edmund what his wife's name was, he said it was Lily!" said Iris as she told the story to the swim group. "Our Lily! Her husband is a hero! Can you believe that?" The group responded with a loud applause and splashing in the pool!

Iris had also interviewed the Police Chief, who referred to Edmund's effort as "The most superhuman surfboard rescue act the world had ever seen!" As a matter of fact, after Edmund's miraculous feat, the U.S. Lifeguards began to use surfboards in their water rescues. Of course, the swim group had all talked about how wonderful he was and that they could hardly wait to talk with Lily.

Lily had been so busy with the twins that she never saw the article and didn't even know what a hero her husband was. Edmund was also so overwhelmed with the babies that he simply never mentioned it.

The Wednesday that Lily returned to the swim group, everyone was so happy to see her, especially Iris. That Wednesday, for the first time Lily learned from her swim group that her amazing husband was also an incredible hero. She was not surprised at all, but was very grateful.

****

"Oh Edmund, I am so proud of you!" Lily said as she hugged her husband when he walked into their house that evening. "Why didn't you tell me about the lives you saved? I can only imagine all the relief and comfort you brought to those families!"

The swim group was getting very close these days. There was so much sharing and talking lately. They had learned many personal things about each other's lives.

It was not uncommon for the women after the class to be greeted by Silas and Sophie, Candace's twins, as they were ready to head home after working in the flower shop with Aunt Vivien.

"Is that a light outside?" asked Candace as she walked past the pool window.

"I see it, but I'm not sure where it's coming from," said Rose. "I actually noticed it a few weeks ago and wondered the same thing."

"I think it's like a reflection or something," said Iris.

"They say that the light always shines in the darkness," whispered Sunny, "and we all know that's true. Saint Francis knew what he was talking about!"

"Well, whatever it is, it's beautiful," said Silas as he too, could see the light.

"Well, whatever it is, it's beautiful," repeated Sophie. Everyone smiled and laughed as Silas rolled his eyes.

Chapter 35

Iris & Mark

Iris had decided to put up flyers around North Beach to open up her church group meetings to the entire community. The group was continuing to dwindle, and she was fearful that she would soon be hosting herself and nobody else if things continued this way.

"Hello, Iris Gabriel!" Mark Fite called from up on top of his ladder in the main room of the library. His new job was keeping him busy, but he always enjoyed seeing Iris.

"Oh, hi, Mark. How are you these days?" responded Iris. "And how is your father doing?" She asked hesitantly. She was really hoping that Mark's father hadn't passed away.

"Let me come down off this ladder and we can go into the break room to talk," he replied. Iris' heart began to beat rapidly. She said a secret prayer to herself that Mark's father was okay.

As the two of them sat down and shyly started talking, Mark took Iris' hand and said, "You are never going to believe this, my dear. My father is doing amazingly well! In fact, I recently moved out of my parents' home for the second time and back into my own apartment! Apparently, according to the doctors, we have witnessed a miracle!

He is back to normal and seems to be cancer-free. We are all taking one day at a time and enjoying life more than ever."

Iris couldn't help the tears that began to roll down her cheeks. "Oh, Mark, I am so happy for you and your mother! Treasure your time together."

****

Mark was truly happy, but he also felt the sadness that Iris was experiencing as she reminisced on a time when she, too, had hoped for a miraculous healing for Cora. They sat in silence for what seemed like an hour, but was only a few minutes. It was insightful of Mark to know that he had to bring Iris into the break room to give her this news. This was an example of what a truly perceptive relationship they had.

"What are you up to today?" Mark said breaking the silence.

Iris quickly shook off her sorrow as though it was a scarf on her shoulder and responded by telling Mark about her church group.

"Oh, that sounds like something I would now have time for. Can I come?" he asked.

"Oh, sure Mark, I would love to have you come," Iris handed him a flyer. "I'll see you on Monday!" she said, and practically ran out of the library.

What have I done now? Iris asked herself, the old feeling of excitement starting to return. She had often thought to herself that Mark was a very nice man and that he might make a nice companion. *This might be good for me,* she answered herself.

Chapter 36

Rose

The holidays had come and gone just as quickly as Rose's hope that her mother would be healed of the cancer that was progressing in her frail body. Rose knew in her heart that she would never spend another Christmas with her mom and had made a special effort to visit her as often as possible. After all, she needed to read to her. They had already finished *Red Shoes for Nancy* and were halfway through *Borrowed Angel*.

The concept of the phrase, 'the last time' was becoming a reality for both Rose and her mother. They could see it in each other's eyes, though their eyes rarely met during her visits. There were times when Rose would feel a sob building up in her chest as she read, and would then wonder if her mother had noticed because her voice would change and become weak. As Rose walked quietly towards the back room where Carmelita was napping, she noticed that *Borrowed Angel* was on the kitchen table next to a large magnifying glass. Oh, my goodness, someone has been cheating, thought Rose as she smiled.

"Hello, Mom, how are you feeling today?" she asked Carmelita.

"So- so. I'm doing fine. How are you, Rosita? Busy, busy, I'm sure, because you never slow down *mija*," said her mom.

"I'm fine, Mom. I thought I would stop by to read a few chapters to you. Do you want to go outside and sit on the porch? I'll grab your sweater and the book. Oh, and we won't be needing the magnifying glass!" she said, giggling afterwards.

"Oh Rosita, you caught me! I was so anxious last night to find out if Nancy got a healing in Lourdes that I tried reading *Borrowed Angel* with a magnifying glass. I'm sorry," she said sadly.

"Don't be sorry Mom, I'm not the book police and besides, I'm going to read to you forever," said Rose as she hid her tears. Deep inside, Rose knew that her mom would die soon. In fact, it was only one week after they finished reading *Borrowed Angel* that her mom did die.

Rose would always treasure those special memories with Carmelita. They would bring her great comfort in the years to come. She even had a photo of the two of them sitting outside on the porch as she read to her. She would carry that photo with her and look at it occasionally to prove to herself that it had really happened. Pictures helped with recalling memories and feelings. Rose felt proud to share the photo with the swim class, especially with Iris, who had been her hero for finding the book. She would be forever grateful to her. Without realizing it, Iris had been responsible for helping develop the close bond Rose had shared with her mother before her death.

****

Losing Jacob and her mom couldn't prepare Rose for the pain she was to endure in the near future. Things were heating up in the United States during the Depression. People were on edge, and everyone felt it. That was part of why Rose continued to perform as a vocalist at Jazz at JuJu's. It was her way of bringing a little joy to people through music. Perhaps it would take their minds off their problems, if only for a few hours. One of her favorite songs was a tune by Louis Armstrong entitled *What a Wonderful World*. It was short, simple, and to the point. If only people could get along with each other.

Chapter 37

Patrick's favorite source of entertainment was the now-famous 'traveling yo-yo.' Vivien's son was a master yo-yo spinner, and his younger brother Daniel often bragged about this. He adored Patrick and talked about him all the time. Patrick could do no wrong in Daniel's world. Vivien and her husband Steven were very proud of their boys and grateful for the time they spent together as a family. The days seemed to regain their joy when, as a family, they could remember Grandpa Ino in a happy way. This, of course, took time and never took the place of the times that were for tears. Everyone understood that crying was just as important as laughing.

Vivi often recalled the story of how her father had never believed in suitcases. "He simply refused to pack for any upcoming trip that we would go on when I was little!"

Theresa, of course, was appalled and embarrassed whenever they would travel to visit her family in Point Lobos. It simply drove her crazy!

"Well, where would he put his clothes, Mom?" asked Patrick.

"Oh, well, he would wear them, Patrick," said Vivi matter-of-factly.

"What? I don't understand."

"My dad — your grandfather — would wear sometimes up to three shirts and three pairs of socks at the same time! Then each day, he would take off the top shirt and pair of socks and be as he would say, 'Fresh as new and ready for the day!' Grandma Theresa thought he was crazy, but what could she do?"

The family felt at peace when they could recall funny stories about Inocencio. It was their way of keeping him alive in their hearts. He had truly made a lasting impression on each of them, and they simply refused to let that go. In fact, every time they came across a pile of dirty clothes they would yell out, "Grandpa Inocencio!"

Chapter 38

Rose: One More Tragedy

It was Saturday night, and Rose had just returned from her great-grandson Alyn's first birthday party. It was almost impossible to imagine that so many people were there to celebrate. Her entire extended family was there, except for her oldest son, Joseph. That was very unusual and had Rose fairly concerned, but she was so distracted by the crowd that she put her 'worry thoughts' out of her mind.

Rose quickly got dressed and dashed out the door to catch a trolley to the club. "I can't be late, I'm already in trouble for not going to the pre-show practice!" She shouted as she ran out. Rose knew how the band leader felt about band members who were late. "No respect," he was always saying.

As the trolley slowed down about half a block away from the club, Rose jumped off and squinted her eyes. Something was very wrong at the club. She could see three Model A police cars blocking the entrance to the club. *What now?* she thought. Last month there had been a big fight in the bar area that caused lots of problems. As Rose came closer to the club, she saw her younger son James.

"Mom..." said James when he saw her.

"What are you doing here, James? What's going on? Why are the police here?" asked Rose. Her heart felt as though it was beating a million times a minute. She felt short of breath. Even before he could explain what was going on, Rose could tell by the look on his face that death had come to visit once again.

"There was a fight in the club, Mom, and well, it's Joseph. Mom, he's gone," James said as he cried. Joseph was Rose's oldest son. James bravely held his mother in his arms as she collapsed. The two of them sobbed uncontrollably. It was almost as though they felt the pain of losing Jacob and Carmelita all over again in addition to losing Joseph. It was like a triple grief.

"This is impossible!" screamed Rose. "I can't take it, this is too much!"

"Mom! You will be okay! I promise, Mom. I will take care of you. We will be okay...." said Jacob between sobs. In his heart, he knew that it would be a very long time before he felt even close to being 'okay,' whatever that was. This marked the beginning of one of the hardest roads James had ever gone down. To lose both of his brothers was brutal to his heart. He felt as though the ground under him was caving in and there was nothing he could do about it. His life was caving in. The huge responsibility of emotionally supporting his mother and other family members seemed downright impossible.

Rose failed to show up to the swim group the next week. The other ladies were speechless when Iris painfully informed them of Rose's son's death.

Iris worked with the reporter who had covered the story, and knew more details than she wished. Apparently, Rose's son had been planning on surprising Rose at the club. He went early and snuck in the back door so as to get a good seat. Unfortunately, there were a few guys inside the club who had been drinking all day and were drunk out of their minds and causing trouble. When Joseph went into the club, the police were outside trying to figure out what was going on. Suddenly, one of the drunk guys grabbed a gun from behind the bar and started shooting towards the police, but shot Joseph instead. It was a horrible, senseless tragedy that had ended Rose's son's life.

"How will we bury another son?" Rose asked her ex-husband. "This can't be happening! What did we do to deserve this? It feels like we are being punished for something!"

"I have no answers for you, Rose. I have tried to be a good person all my life. I don't know what to say," he said, sadly looking down and shaking his head.

Chapter 39

Is there a limit to how much pain one heart can endure? The swim class was very quiet that cloudy morning the ladies met. Iris could not imagine how Rose would survive losing Joseph after her other son and mother had died. She and the other women in the group, together with Candace, cried tears of agony and pain. They all loved Rose dearly and wanted somehow to help their friend. They all worried that it would be a long time before they would see Rose again. The pain that each individual felt was united with Rose's unthinkable loss. Even though they all had plenty of practice weeping silently, today they cried together out loud.

Candace wanted desperately to help Rose, but had no idea what to do. In her insightful way, she knew that the important thing right now was to steadily allow the women to cry and grieve openly for their friend. They all shared a bond with each other and soon would be able to find the strength and courage they needed to actively support Rose.

After the sobbing diminished, Iris broke the silence with her decision. "I'd like to have a pot-luck dinner at my house next Tuesday night for Rose. I think having a meal together might be good for her."

"That sounds like a great idea. I can bring a salad," said Lily.

"I can bring a pecan pie," added Sunny.

****

The following day, Iris was suprised to find a message on her desk from Rose. The message said that she planned to see all of them at the swim class next week. Iris knew that the best thing to do was to allow Rose to lead the way in her grief, so she canceled the pot-luck and informed the group that Rose would be coming to the class at the pool on Wednesday.

****

Meanwhile, at the Sanchez home, it was impossible to keep the recent tragedy from Silas and Sophie. They knew about everything that happened in San Francisco, and it was just as well. Hiding death from children was not something Theresa or her family believed in.

"We are all going to die someday, and somehow we need to learn how to face that in our daily living. We must teach our children about death while at the same time we focus on life. You can't have one without the other." Theresa would say.

"I have been planning to do something special for your swim class, Mommy," said Silas.

"I have been planning to do something special for your swim class, Mommy," mimicked Sophie.

"Can we come to class on Wednesday?" they both asked in unison.

"Why of course you can!" replied Candace.

"I would also like to attend your class, Candace. Is that okay?" said Theresa.

Everyone in the room was shocked. Candace paused as she looked over at Vivi.

"Oh Mom, If you really feel up to it," said Candace. "You can bring the twins," she added.

"Well, I was thinking that maybe I could go to the swim class and then work in the flower shop in the afternoon," she said shyly.

Candace and Vivien both looked at each other, shocked, and then smiled. They had wanted this for so long. It was like a dream coming true in the midst of a tragedy. More tears welled up in everyone's eyes. Their mother had endured so much loss in her life and certainly could benefit from the group's love and support. She didn't fear loss and had a great insight into survival, and could definitely share her experiences with the other women.

Chapter 40

Iris: Moving

Iris felt confident that her life was about to change as she hammered the 'For Sale' sign into the soft, wet dirt in the front yard. The large house that had once been home to five people was just too big for her now. Even when the kids were with her every other week, it was still too big. So many dreams had faded for Iris, and living in that house was feeling very lonely for her. "We can create new memories in another house," she carefully explained to the children as she told them of her plans to sell it.

Now came the task of convincing herself of that! She was still not sure how she would be able to leave the only house Cora had lived in. She worried that the memories they had created in that home would be left behind to be forgotten. This certainly wasn't an easy step, she thought as she stared at the painting of Cora in the front room.

No! The memories will go with me in my heart, she told herself. But how would she manage that? She considered setting up a room in the new house for Cora's things, but quickly dismissed that idea. That would be too strange, and simply not the same. Nothing she or anyone could ever do would bring back Cora.

As the weeks passed and she carefully packed each room, she felt more and more confident that Cora, and her love for her, was deep in her soul and nothing would ever take or disturb that.

"Iris, if it's alright, I think you should take down the painting of Cora. I'm afraid I might drop it and I would never forgive myself if it became damaged," said Mark.

"Oh Mark, you are so silly. I think you can handle a painting, and besides, you are stronger than I am!" said Iris. "Thanks again, by the way, for helping me with this move. I really needed the help."

The painting of Cora at the piano would undoubtedly hang in the front room of the new home because it always prompted questions from visitors who had never met Cora. Iris loved explaining who her precious daughter had been. At first, it was painful to realize that there were people in her life who had never known Cora, but then just saying her name again brought a special feeling to her heart. Iris empowered herself when she described her daughter's inner and outer beauty.

The move to a new house would be hard but it was the right thing to do. It would be proof that Cora could never be left behind. Her everlasting love and amazing memories would be moving along together with each of them. Iris would hold every moment sacred with her children, as she knew the true meaning of the saying, "No one is promised tomorrow." Erin and Vanessa both adored Iris. Laughing together and being silly together united them in a very special way. Iris was so gentle with each of them as they approached problems in everyday living. The three of them all knew the courage it would take to move.

Chapter 41

Candace and the twins arrived early at Vivien's house as the thick fog from the bay crept in that Wednesday. Silas had insisted that they go early to prepare the flower shop for his grandmother's first day back. The night before, there was definitely something on his mind. As Candace poured herself a cup of coffee in Vivien's spotless kitchen, she said, "I don't know what that child is up to! It bothers me that he can keep a secret so well. I thought I knew everything about my children, but apparently not!" She was so upset that morning that she almost spilled her coffee.

"Well, he has been wandering off when we are at the flower shop, but honestly, he is so helpful. I wouldn't worry too much, Candace. Our

161

children have their own minds and we have to accept that. I know it's hard, but as much as we want to, we can't always control their worlds," said Vivi sadly.

"Let's get going ladies, we have work to do!" said Silas.

"Let's get going ladies, we have work to do!" repeated Sophie.

"I suppose coffee time is over..." mumbled Candace.

"By the way, where is Mom?" asked Vivi. "I thought you were bringing her to class today."

"Oh, sorry Vivi, I forgot to tell you that you're supposed to meet her at the trolley station on Geary Street at 8:30. I hope that's okay. She was still getting ready when I stopped by this morning, and I didn't dare rush her," said Candace.

"Sure, that's fine. I was worried she had changed her mind about going. After all, she's been stuck in her grief for a long time and this must be difficult for her," said Vivien.

Meanwhile, back at Theresa's house, she was experiencing something she had forgotten all about. It was a touch of happiness. It felt strange to her. She recognized the old feeling, but was almost afraid to feel it completely. Was it disrespectful to be happy after the love of her life died? That thought haunted her. Her life had been so fixed in the pain from the past that she had almost dismissed her happiness completely.

As she looked around her house that morning, she couldn't help but realize that her family needed her. Especially her grandchildren. All four of them adored her and would do anything to see her smile again and laugh with them. Sharing happiness was true love, just as sharing sorrow was also love, but somehow those two experiences had become unbalanced in their lives. It was time to amend that and she was ready.

I think I'll pack some cover-alls and one of Ino's old shirts today, she thought to herself. *The flower shop needs some cleaning and I want to be prepared.*

She also packed one of the bathing suits she had purchased years ago with the best of intentions, but had never worn. The one thing that Theresa did not have to pack was Inocencio's dream of healing from grief. It was imbedded deep in her heart, and now she knew that through her gentle spirit, she was about to become a part of making Ino's dream come true for the swim group.

Theresa was also concerned about meeting the ladies in Candace's swim group. When she learned early on from Candace that the ladies had all lost children, she had begun to secretly pray for each of them daily. Although she had never lost a child, she never forgot about what it was like to witness her mother's pain from losing her son, Rudy. Prayer was her way of helping. She firmly believed in it!

As Theresa cautiously stepped off the trolley, Vivi was there to greet her. "Happy Wednesday, Mom!" she said sweetly.

"Oh Vivien, you are so silly. It's just another day," Theresa replied. But Vivien knew in her heart that this day was special. Something wonderful was in the air today and she couldn't hold back her smile.

164

Chapter 42

Lily

Lily didn't mind the fog in San Francisco as long as it lifted by noon. On dark days like this, she felt very cozy and somehow it seemed like she had extra time to begin the day with the twins. Edmund had found a very reliable babysitter named Yolanda who could handle the girls quite well. She was a college student from Iowa who came from a large family and had lots of experience with children. Yolanda's patience with them was everything they desired.

"I'd like to leave early today, as I want to go by the flower shop to talk with Candace before the swim group," she said to Yolanda.

"Sure, that's fine," said Yolanda.

"I want to talk to Candace because she has been raising twins, and I need advice from someone who really knows what it's like," said Lily as though she was talking to herself. "I worry that I'm not a good mother and I need advice."

Lily often doubted herself when issues came up with the girls. It was hard to give them the attention they demanded. Sometimes it felt as if the day was gone by the time they had breakfast and were dressed for the day. Candace always seemed so calm and organized. Lily was beginning to think that it was more than not having her mother around to help, and so wanted to talk with Candace and get some ideas from her. She often felt impatient with the girls and didn't know why. Her anger was getting the best of her and she felt bad. *Maybe my expectations of the twins are too high. I just need to talk to someone who might understand me...*she thought silently to herself.

She smiled as she checked her watch. Once again, she felt her mother's presence when she looked at the watch and vividly remembered her mother giving it to her for her eighteenth birthday. She had an hour before the class, and hopefully, Candace would be there.

****

Lily reached her destination, the flower shop at the Sanchez Bath House.

"Good morning, Lily. It's so nice to see you," said Candace as she worked on two bouquets of flowers for Rose. It was sad to imagine that now Rose had two sons to grieve for. Candace had taken it upon herself to prepare a bouquet for each of them.

"And a good morning to you, Candace. I'm so glad you are here, and I hope it's okay that I am here so early," Lily replied.

The remaining hour before class evolved into a wonderful and meaningful discussion about raising twins. Lily was able to finally express her feelings with someone who had experience and understood.

"Thank you so much for your wisdom and insight, Candace. I so appreciate talking with you. I feel so much better. I was actually starting to feel like I was the worst mother in the world!" Lily said.

"Oh, no, Lily, we continue to learn as we move forward in life. No one is exempt from problems and difficulties when raising children. Vivien and I were just this morning discussing raising children. I recently read in a book by Kahlil Gibran, 'Your children are not your children. They are the sons and daughters of Life's longing for itself.' It's so true, don't you think?" asked Candace.

"I had never really thought about it but, yes, it is true. I don't own my daughters, I am simply here to guide them in the best way I know how," replied Lily. "I just don't want to make any mistakes!" It was hard to separate her feelings because so much of her life always pointed back to losing her mom and Liana. She struggled with what was simply frustration in raising the girls or left-over feelings of grief over her huge loss.

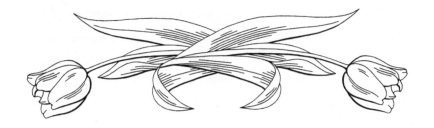

Chapter 43

Theresa clutched her bag tightly where she had packed her swimsuit. Her heart was beating fast and doubt was creeping into her mind. *I think I have made a huge mistake by coming today,* she thought to herself. *I don't think I'm ready.* On the other hand, she also knew that sometimes not feeling ready was unimportant, and so she continued to simply put one foot in front of the other and carry on. Ino was no longer here to make her decisions for her and she had to be brave and do it herself. Life was moving forward, with or without her. It would take every ounce of courage that she possessed to go back to the flower shop and attend the swim class today.

"Ladies, I hope this is okay with you, but we have a new member in our swim group!" said Candace. Once again, there were no echoes in the pool room. The 'sacred silence' was there to stay; such a strange phenomenon. Theresa quietly walked into the poolroom staying close to Candace.

"Her name is Theresa, and she runs the flower shop upstairs. And she happens to be Vivien's and my mother! Vivien has been taking care of the shop since the death of my father, but now my mother is back, and she would also like to join our swim class!" Candace found herself holding back tears. Sunny, Iris, and Lily clapped their hands in delight!

"Welcome, Theresa! We would love for you to join us. Your daughters are such sweet and kind women and now we know why!" Sunny said.

The next half hour was filled with introductions and small talk. Candace noticed that Rose had not arrived. Meanwhile, her son James had arrived upstairs at the flower shop to pick up the bouquet for Jacob that Candace had prepared. He didn't seem surprised at all that she had taken it upon herself to prepare two bouquets, one for Jacob's grave and the other for Joseph's funeral. James mentioned that his mother was busy preparing for the upcoming funeral. He gave Vivien the details of the services as his mother had instructed him. James would do anything for his mother, as he knew all too well the pain she felt at this time. His own heart felt a tremendous amount of pain too. He had lost another brother and that simply broke his already shattered heart. It wasn't easy being the only surviving son his parents had.

The swim class soon realized that Rose hadn't shown up for class and sadly acknowledged her absence.

"I think we should go together to Rose's son's funeral service," said Lily. "I think she might want us to be there."

"Yes, the services are, after all, for the living," said Iris. "She certainly needs our support, and reaching out to her in this way is the right thing to do." Iris had never been much for attending funerals, but after Cora died, she understood how important it was to see her friends and family join together to honor her daughter.

Theresa was impressed at how loving the group was when discussing Rose's recent tragedy. She sensed deep respect within the group. She had worried that they would all be focused on her as the new member, but the distraction caused by Rose's absence and situation helped take the spotlight off of her.

She had immediately noticed the absence of echoes in the pool room, but kept it to herself. She took it as an added bonus to her excitement of being a part of a group. This was new for her and she liked it!

Right before class was about to end, Theresa's precious grandchildren and Vivien entered the pool area. Silas and Sophie held beautiful flowers in each of their little hands as they walked hesitantly towards the ladies in the pool.

"We have a surprise for you ladies," said Silas, filled with excitement.

"We have a surprise for you ladies," added Sophie sweetly.

Candace's eyes overflowed with tears. *So that's what he's been planning!* she realized. Sure enough, they held the most beautiful roses, lilies, sunflowers, irises, and tulips that any of them had ever seen. An amazing, breathtaking ambience filled the room. None of them felt any pain or sorrow only peace, and it was stunning!

The twins had been planning this ever since Silas had taken notice of the ladies' names. Together with Vivien's help, they pulled it off. Silas's idea had been to give each of the ladies a small bouquet that contained one rose, one lily, one sunflower, and one iris. He just couldn't get over the fascination that all of their names were also the names of flowers. He had talked to Vivien about this constantly.

"It's just like some kind of miracle, Auntie Vivi!"

When they heard that their grandmother would be joining the group, it was Sophie's idea to add a tulip to each bouquet. It has long been known that tulips are associated with true, perfect love. That was how they both saw their grandmother, as someone who gave them the perfect love that they all needed.

Chapter 44

Sunny & Lily: At the Funeral

"I'm going to a funeral this morning, Danny, and I was hoping you would be able to pick up Martin from school," Sunny said as she fumbled through several pairs of high heels in her closet. It had been a long time since she had been dressed up, and she had a particular pair in mind for that day.

"Sure, I'll be home for the next few days since we've closed the case we've been working on," he answered. Danny took his job very seriously and did everything in his power to solve problems. "Whose funeral are you going to?"

"Well, one of the ladies in my swim group lost her son. He was murdered at Jazz at JuJu's," she said sadly.

"Oh yes, that case is complicated. It may never be solved. I'm not on it, but I know it's been a nightmare for the family and the local police," said Danny. "Do you want me to go with you?"

"No, I'm fine. I just need you to pick up Martin. Please don't forget."

Both Danny and Sunny worried about their younger son. He was so quiet and never talked much after Brandon died. They wanted him to share his feelings, but it was clear that he was not willing to do that yet. He refused to even say Brandon's name. It was almost as though he was angry at him for leaving the family in such a shocking way. He'd had a front row seat to the damage it had done to both of his parents and he couldn't understand why it happened. He was unique in his grieving because he was the only one who saw the pain in his parents every day, not to mention his own pain over losing the brother who he had thought had hung the moon and the stars and could do no wrong. Brandon had been here one day and simply gone the next. It was a shocking and tragic loss.

Martin had lots of friends at school, but none of them had ever experienced what he had. It isolated him, in a way, and created a sense of hidden anger. At the same time, he was a teenager, and that in itself created so many strange new emotions in his life.

Sunny sensed Martin's anger, but never spoke to him about it for fear of upsetting him more. She wasn't willing to take the chance of any conflict, something she never used to fear. Sunny was always the one who stood tall in her high heels and the meticulous suits she wore, and she never shied away from conversations.

Sunny and Danny remained totally aware of Martin's actions, and were careful to be there for him whenever he needed them. Their families did whatever they could to support them. Sometimes that was just by listening to Sunny talk about Brandon.

People were forever asking how they could help, but the truth was, the Andersons had no idea what they needed or wanted. They had never lost a son before, so how were they supposed to know what they needed?

****

"Hello, Lily! I'm glad I saw you. I was afraid I was at the wrong church! North Beach has several Cathedral-like churches and I was worried that I would mix them up," announced Sunny.

"Oh, I know what you mean!" replied Lily. "I felt a bit lost this morning myself."

"Of course, that's not unusual for me..." Sunny nodded and smiled as she gently closed her eyes for a second.

She suddenly remembered a booklet she had come across the year before, at Christmas time. "Lily, have you ever read *Handling the Holidays* by Bruce Conley? It's a booklet about what to do during those times that are next to impossible to get through. I know that baby Liana died during Christmas time just like my Brandon."

"No, I've never heard of it, but I'd like to see it if you have a copy. Maybe it would help," replied Lily.

"I'm thinking of decorating my Christmas tree next year with sunflowers! The booklet suggests that you try to remember your loved ones during the holidays instead of drowning in your despair all by yourself," said Sunny.

"I think that's a wonderful idea, Sunny! Please invite me over to see your tree when you decorate! I can't think of a better way to spend the hardest time of the year," Lily said as the two of them approached the church.

Chapter 45

Rose

It was almost a ritual Rose performed before she went anywhere, that she changed clothes at least four times. I don't know how I will get through this day, she thought over and over again. Facing her family and friends would be comforting yet exhausting at the same time. She sometimes felt as though she had to comfort them just as much as they comforted her. Each of the losses she had felt in her life seemed to be taking more and more out of her. She felt lifeless at times. It was as though she was becoming numb to any pain, and at the same time feeling the worst pain ever. She had become stuck between the past and the future, as though she was a separate person within herself. "I wish I could just run away," had become one of her favorite secret wishes.

Meanwhile, Rose's father, Eduardo, had arrived early to accompany her to Joseph's funeral.

"You are stronger than you realize, *mija*," he repeated several times to her throughout the day. "I know you, and I will be here right by your side. I'm not going anywhere too soon, Rosita. In fact, I pray to God to give me at least one more year on earth to help you get through this," he said lovingly. "Our littlest fella, Alyn, needs you, Rosita."

The ladies from the swim group, including Candace and Vivien, were all waiting outside St. Peter and St. Paul Church in North Beach. The ladies all felt a very strong empathy for Rose. Theresa gently wiped her tears as she reminisced about Inocencio's funeral at the same church. This time the tears were for Rose and her family. Theresa knew the depth of her own pain, but couldn't imagine losing a son or daughter. She reminded herself of the many years she had together with Inocencio, and was grateful for that time. Some of these women only had their children for a few years. The more she thought about it, the more grateful she felt. This powerful feeling of gratitude seemed to almost melt her sorrow away.

That morning, Silas had asked Candace if she would take the bouquet that he and Sophie had prepared for Rose to the funeral and give it to her. Candace thanked him and decided that it was a great idea. Silas was determined to bring peace and tranquility to others through the beauty of flowers. His grandmother Theresa had taught him that.

Chapter 46

The Funeral & The Never-Ending Fruitcake

The flowers that Candace held tightly in her small hands appeared more beautiful than they had when Silas first handed the bouquet to his mother.

"Please give these to Rose and be sure to tell her that me and Sophie made the bouquet for her," Silas had said that morning. He couldn't help but wonder if the ladies would notice the choice of flowers they had made when preparing the bouquets with Vivien. It was an interesting combination of flowers, similar to the different personalities of the group. Perhaps it was life's way of telling people that despite our differences, we are all so beautiful together.

As Rose turned to walk out of the church after the service, she spotted her dear friends from the swim group.

"They came," she whispered to herself. "My friends came."

An overwhelming sense of appreciation filled her heart, and suddenly the day became easier. She had just hours ago called it the loneliest day of her life. Now it felt as though having her friends beside her to share her sorrow lightened the new burden of grief. It gave her hope. They didn't have to say a word, and they all knew that. Their silent presence defined the love they all had for their dear friend.

As Rose approached them, Candace handed her the bouquet. She smiled through her tears and took the bouquet. It was all she needed to get through another painful loss in her life. Holding the bouquet that Silas and Sophie had prepared gave her strength and courage. One rose, one sunflower, one lily, one iris, and a tulip.

"I plan on going to class soon," Rose whispered. "I miss you. Hey, what about joining us for a reception after the services today? It's in the church classrooms next door. I would love for all of you to come."

****

Theresa, Vivien, and Candace all sat together with the ladies from the swim group at the reception. Together, they seemed to Rose to represent an extraordinary strength. They all knew first-hand how it felt to lose someone you loved.

"I hope you don't mind ladies, but I have a funny story about a funeral I attended last year," announced Iris, her voice shaky but confident.

"Oh, please share it with us," piped up Sunny. "We need funny!"

"Well, it was Christmas time and, of course, baking was occurring all over San Francisco. We had invited my brother and his wife over for dinner the night before we attended the funeral of a distant relative of mine. My sister-in-law had brought a rather large fruit cake over for the dinner. It was probably at least two feet long! I had never seen one like it!"

"Anyway, the next day when it came time to leave for the funeral, I thought to myself, 'I should take the remainder of the fruitcake to the reception after the funeral today...' I quickly cut the cake to make it even and re-wrapped it in waxed paper."

"When we arrived at the reception, I handed it to one of the servers and began to mingle. The gathering was similar to this one, where everyone shared a meal together. It seemed to lighten the mood," continued Iris.

"Several days later, I invited some relatives that I had seen at the reception over for dinner. I hadn't seen them in a few years. That evening, in walked my cousin Nena with a fruitcake! The same fruitcake that my sister-in-law had brought me and that I took to the funeral! Just like every family knows the legend about the fruitcake that makes its rounds, my fruitcake had come back! I immediately began to laugh and, of course, had to explain my behavior to my guests!"

The group, including Rose and her father, burst into laughter. This may have seemed odd to other people at the reception, but everyone at that table was certainly okay with laughter as a way of healing. Rose felt very comfortable with her friends, and went on to tell a few other funny stories about her sons (or 'fellas' as her dad referred to them). It was a hard, but healing afternoon.

Chapter 47

The women continued to meet each Wednesday for years to come. Theresa's fear of the water began to dissipate. She started slowly by simply sitting at the side of the pool and kicking her feet in the water. The echoing sound, typical of pool areas, was never heard in the room while the women met. Theresa believed that the echo had moved itself into Sophie, as she never stopped echoing what Silas said! Every so often, a beautiful light entered the room from an unknown source and someone was always there to take notice.

Silas and Sophie tended to the explosion of flowers that had started to grow naturally all along the back area of the pool. They were Linnaea borealis, or 'twin flowers,' as they are better known. Silas had cried the first time he laid eyes on them.

"These are God's gifts to Sophie and me," he would tell people.

Meanwhile, back home in her upstairs library, Theresa started reading some of Inocencio's favorite books. This brought great joy to her because only she could understand why he had held such a passion for the books.

Candace and Vivien continued to be busy, as usual, especially with the grand opening of Candace and Vivien's Care Package Shop on the main strip of Fisherman's Wharf. Each Saturday on their way to work at the Care Package Shop, they would meet at Freddie's Sandwiches on the corner of Francisco Street and Stockton in North Beach. They sold sourdough bread sandwiches for ten cents! The pastrami was the best in all of California!

****

Rose convinced her grandson, Alyn, to take piano lessons and he eventually joined the band and played alongside her at Jazz at JuJu's. Music was her release and gave her the freedom to express herself. Her only living son, James, became an airline pilot for TWA, and often whispered words to his two brothers and grandparents, who he felt closer to when he was flying at 40,000 feet. He never let Rose down and supported her for the rest of their lives.

****

Lily, Edmund, and their twin daughters opened up Liana's Pastry Shop in Nob Hill one Christmas Eve. They learned how to make the most delicious almond croissants on the face of the earth. They were so good

184

that people came from all over California to taste them. It was rumored that some individuals would cry tears of joy as they ate them.

****

Sunny and Danny continued to spend quality time with their boys and their families. They opened up a small business that specialized in sunflowers. Brandon's son, Luke, became the manager of the business and sold the seeds as bird food to local pet shops.

****

Despite the fact that she was four inches taller, Iris and Mark were married on August 29th,1930. Years later, Iris' son, Erin, opened up The Orchid House on Market Street. It was a place for people who needed temporary housing during hard times. Erin had always been very sensitive to the needs of poor people, and was dedicated to helping them. Both Iris and Mark published many books, which remain in stock in the People's Library.

****

Candace, Vivien, and Theresa couldn't help but feel Inocencio's presence every time they saw the healing transpiring in each of the woman as they learned to enjoy life again. It was a dream come true, and they all felt it.

Time was passing by with great speed. Events continued to take place in each of the women's lives; weddings, birthdays, baby showers, graduations, funerals — you name it. They all moved along, embracing life, but never forgetting their children. That was impossible. Yes, some memories began to fade, but never the love they had in their hearts for the children. That evolved into an amazing, strong sense of gratitude

185

for their children. They continued to always be grateful that they had been chosen to be: Liana's mother, Cora's mother, Brandon's mother, and Jacob and Joseph's mother. Supporting each other also taught them to be forever grateful for their friendship.

Rose, Lily, Sunny, and Iris learned that small acts of kindness, laughter, gentle hugs, patience, and prayers are all essential to surviving grief. They had all felt how important it was to let go of guilt. They learned that distractions help ease the intensity of sadness, and that the one true thing that replaces sorrow is gratitude.

Epilogue

Rose

Rosie lives in Albuquerque, New Mexico, and continues her career as a vocalist in the Salsa band, Cafe Mocha. She spends countless hours babysitting for her son Lee's grandson, Alyn (her great-grandson). When you walk into her home, you can truly feel the presence of both Patrick and Lee. Their handsome smiles can be seen in the carefully framed pictures on the walls.

Lily

Nancy is a clinical research manager and has been a very important part of the research done at the UNM Pediatric Oncology Department. Her husband Edmund is a theoretical physicist at Sandia Labs in New Mexico. He loves to surf and wind surf. They are both very busy parents raising two beautiful daughters, Olivia and Naomi, who are not twins. Not a day goes by that Nancy does not miss her mother, Susan. Christmas is still difficult for both of them as they will never forget the year they lost their first daughter, Liana.

Sunny

Susan lives in Claremont, California and is a very successful certified realtor. Her husband, Danny, is a deputy sheriff and works as a flight paramedic for the LA County Sheriff's Department. They spend as much time as possible caring for Brandon's son, Luke. Susan and Danny and their family are involved in raising money to help prevent suicide. Each year on Brandon's birthday they, coordinate a program to feed the homeless in their area. In their living room is a beautiful bronze urn in the shape of the Pieta, which contains Brandon's ashes. Brandon is forever remembered in their hearts.

Iris

Janis, originally from Chicago, is a pediatrician in Santa Fe, New Mexico, working currently as the Bureau Chief, Medical Director, and Title V Maternal Child Health Director – Family Health Bureau, NM Department of Health. She has been a true advocate for children's health issues for over twenty years. Her two children are both in college and still manage to spend precious time with Janis, laughing and just being silly together. In the family living room, drawing attention to all who enter, is a painting of a special gift to our world, young Cariana (Cora).

About the Author

Cathy Chavez, a native New Mexican, was born and educated in Albuquerque, New Mexico. After graduating from Valley High School, she attended the University of New Mexico and earned her Bachelor of Science degree in nursing. In 1980, she began her nursing career at the University of New Mexico Children's Hospital. She worked on the pediatric ward until 1983 and then took a job as a Pediatric Oncology Nurse at UNM from 1983 until 2017. Her roles included: Oncology Nurse Specialist, Nurse Manager, and Research Nurse.

Her experiences in nursing include administering chemotherapy to children, hospice work with children and their families, teaching treatment plans, discharge plans and protocols to families, and various other responsibilities. She has co-authored many publications in journals on Pediatric Oncology subjects.

She received her National CPON certification and maintained that throughout her nursing career. She was a member of the NCI funded research group, COG.

Cathy attended Camp Enchantment every summer as the Camp RN from 1986-2016. She also co-directed Sibling Camp Superstars. Ms. Chavez has drawn on her thirty-seven years of experience in working with young people with cancer and their families to produce an insider's look at the dynamics of families dealing with such critical quality-of-life issues.

She is married and has two married daughters and four grandchildren. In her spare time, she attends yoga classes and creates silver and gold jewelry pieces.

Acknowledgments

My inspiration for this novel came from personal experiences in my life and my career as a Pediatric Oncology Nurse. For many years, I have felt a special healing every time I visit the Sutro Bath ruins in San Francisco. I was inspired at the ruins to write this novel.

Though Inocencio Sanchez, his family, and their friends are fictional beings, their stories are based on the memoirs and histories of real people. I would like to commend and thank Rosie Encinias, Nancy Eisenberg, Susan Aleman and Janis Gonzales MD, for courageously allowing me to use their life experiences in this novel. Their encouragement and support with this project made it possible.

I would also like to thank my brother, Rudy Miera, who has believed in me from the very beginning of this project and continues to encourage me through his wisdom and patience. He has helped me find my voice through the written word.

A very heartfelt thank you goes to my husband Ruben and my daughters, Irene and Celina, who have witnessed my true intentions for this novel.

CPSIA information can be obtained
at www.ICGtesting.com
Printed in the USA
FSHW011440120519
58073FS